Faerie

Faerie

EISHA MARJARA

ARSENAL PULP PRESS
VANCOUVER

ARSENAL PULP PRESS
Suite 202 – 211 East Georgia St.
Vancouver, BC V6A 1Z6
Canada
arsenalpulp.com

The publisher gratefully acknowledges the support of the Canada Council for the Arts and the British Columbia Arts Council for its publishing program, and the Government of Canada (through the Canada Book Fund) and the Government of British Columbia (through the Book Publishing Tax Credit Program) for its publishing activities.

Cover photograph: "Head in the Clouds" by Sally Anscombe (Getty Images)
Cover design by Gerilee McBride
Text design by Oliver McPartlin
Edited by Susan Safyan, Robyn So, and Linda Field
Printed and bound in Canada

Library and Archives Canada Cataloguing in Publication
  Marjara, Eisha, author
      Faerie / Eisha Marjara.

  Issued in print and electronic formats.
  ISBN 978-1-55152-618-8 (paperback).—ISBN 978-1-55152-619-5 (epub)

      I. Title.

  PS8626.A75365F34 2015   jC813'.6   C2015-903484-1
                                                    C2015-903485-X:

Faerie

Part One:

Pupa

01. Eighteen

I had a plan, a wish for my eighteenth birthday. I dreamed of leaving the four walls of the hospital behind and living on the generous offerings of winter, of feeding on snowflakes, melting away the last remaining pounds, and withering into oblivion. The numbers *one* and *eight* were terrifying to me; I could not face them. I couldn't fathom the "hoods" of my future—womanhood, adulthood, and most dreadful, however unlikely, motherhood. No matter how I could or would shrink my flesh, I was helpless to nature's most incredible and cruel weapon: time.

Mid-morning in the middle of February, I paced the hallway—as I had many times before—and counted each calorie I burned. On the hundredth, I stationed my sixty-eight pound, five-foot-three frame in front of the hospital's elevator while all official eyes were elsewhere. When the doors opened, I made my escape.

I darted out the main door, tore across the parking lot, and headed straight for late-morning traffic. I began to sing Whitney Houston's "I'm Every Woman" down traffic-jammed Poirier Avenue, past wide eyes and frozen bodies that watched the spectacle of the emaciated, half-naked humanoid in hospital garb trying to make a dim-witted escape from time. I belted the song from the hollow pit of my stomach, but my vocal chords could only produce ghost words, breathless puffs that dissipated into the frigid air. I dashed down the sloping road and into a hazy cloud of exhaust fumes that rose into the heavens and into my lungs. Shuffling through the snow, I went deeper into downtown, where I saw zombie expressions on the faces of commuters and shoppers who, for a moment, stood still as I passed them, attempting to weave a story from this incongruent scene. I could feel my heart pound hard against my thorax and my lungs collapse with each exhalation. Ribs pressing into skin. Throat choking for air.

"Can I help you, miss?" I saw a hand extended, an offer of help that drifted into my indifferent ear, possibly from the man waiting for the ever-late number 199 bus. The pale warmth in my flesh drained quickly into a bloodless blue-grey, my limbs slowed and loosened; I was ready to collapse. *Oh, finally*, I thought. *Finally, this is the absolute end.* The end of me, the end of time as I knew it. Then, when the shock of winter penetrated my bones, my mother's face appeared to me. I froze in the memory of her embrace. I was cured of the fatal rules of time and of weight. And then, I was back in time again. I felt my arm nearly ripped from its socket.

"Stop! You stupid girl! Get back here!" The white coats and residents had caught up. They flung my weary body into an ambulance and dragged it into the loneliest room in the hospital. I kicked and screamed all the way back, losing a fairy tale slipper along the way, and feeling completely the crushing pain of my hideous life and my fear of growing up. One lethal tranquillizer in the ass and I was out like Sleeping Beauty.

02. Problem of Nature

The sting of the injection hadn't worn off. My sunken buttock still throbbed under the bed sheet; a cherry-sized wound stained my underwear with a spot of pink. A hard knot of bluish flesh on my right hamstring felt like a mark of victory for my unheroic attempt to escape Four East. Never in my wildest dreams did I expect to end up here. At seventeen, while my classmates were caught up in drunken parties, first apartments, and debilitating crushes, I was determined to die by starvation.

Four East didn't amount to much. It was a hallway of less than 150 feet on the fourth floor of St Catherine's Hospital. A blue sign hung over the double-door entrance like the gateway to hell: psychiatry. In the dim, narrow rooms, three species roamed: a guard of alert and functioning shift-working specialists; a breed of brooding phantoms plucked from homes and streets and sedated into semi-consciousness until retrieved by family and friends and returned to the insanity that had brought them here; and me, the youngest, smallest, lightest, most unyielding one on the floor.

I was a curious sort, a creature that had been misplaced, although I was half-alive like the rest. The remedy was to be a dreadful and complicated concoction of diet, medication, psychotherapy, behaviour therapy, an overdose of reverse psychology, and gentle electroshock when all else failed. I was a nuisance to the staff and had a reputation as a brat who was butt resistant to any treatment that came my way. At sixty-eight pounds, there wasn't much of me left to treat.

After my escape attempt, staff convened in the nursing station for their daily report, where they declared me "dangerous," and "in contempt of the rules of the ward." Dr Messer's prescription was to intensify my behaviour-modification therapy: "Bed rest and solitary confinement for an indefinite period. Meals in the room, bathroom restricted, no visitors, no phone calls, no reading, no writing, no radio, no talking to anyone except staff." No to every-thing, except meals, when I had to say "yes" to everything, to every morsel of animal, mineral, or vegetable that came on the tray, for every single meal, every single day. Refusing to eat meant only more "no's" on the long list of restrictions.

Because of my unsuccessful attempt to end it all, I'd been ad-mitted into Four East's inner chamber, the PACU. The Patient Acute Care Unit that Acutely Cared for Units like me.

I awoke in a faded yellow room, one of three in this inner sanc-tum, which opened onto a small lounge furnished with a dusty couch, a wicker side table piled with faded women's journals from the last century, and a single battered copy of *Catcher in the Rye* scribbled with notes and comments from a bipolar patient turned outpatient whose room I now occupied. A twenty-four-inch RCA suspended from a high shelf overlooked the scene like the eye of god.

Dr Messer put me on bed rest and in "solitary confinement" (as though the company of two other psychiatric patients was going to be excessively social). My door had to remain closed, except for meal times, and I was not allowed speak with anyone but staff. I was a danger to myself. The worst part was that everything I owned—every book, pen, paper, bottle of shampoo, even my hairpins—had to be locked away. The restrictions imposed upon me made me burn with rage. I could find relief only in acts of carefully executed rebellion.

But I had no weapon with which to fight this losing battle. In a bare room, I had nothing but solemn walls, a creaky bed, a tray table, and a solid wooden door with a small rectangular window through which I could be constantly watched, like a soufflé in the oven. My room's windows opened to the grim inner courtyard facing the E wing. There was a bedpan and a roll of toilet paper. When I needed to go to the bathroom, I had to inform the staff.

On the morning after my attempted escape, I felt drugged and weary until breakfast entered the room in the hands of my new nurse. She was fair-haired, slim, and statuesque. I envisioned Barbie herself, liberating me from these barbaric conditions and about to feed me diet soda and low-fat strawberry Jell-O. Then I noticed that the nurse was not only pregnant but wore a frighteningly stark schoolteacher expression.

"Good morning. I'm Patricia. I'm going be your nurse here at PACU." With a smile, she dropped the meal on to the tray table and whipped it over my gut. "And *this* is your breakfast."

"I'm not eating all that." I flung my arms across my chest.

"Well, then you'll lose more privileges."

I snarled sarcastically. "What privileges are you talking about? My bedpan or the stunning décor in my room?"

"If you're not going to cooperate, Lila, it's only going make things harder for you."

I gave the tray a once-over. "I didn't ask for all this!"

"Excuse me, but you lost that right a long time ago. If you haven't noticed, this is *not* a hotel. You know why you are here." Nurse "Personality" spun on her heels and walked out the door. It smelled like war to me.

I took careful inventory of the food and mentally computed 750 staggering calories. Add the can of Ensure, and it came to 1,000! I felt a delirious panic and pushed away the tray, unable to breathe. Searching for a way out, a way to do away with the calories, I jumped off the bed and paced in my cubicle like a zoo animal, eyes fixed on the tray, collecting my thoughts, calculating calories. I was meant to be on bed rest, so I returned to bed. But I wanted to fling that tray against the room's hideous yellow walls.

As I stared at the food, I summoned all my resolve to combat the rules. I used old and new techniques, harnessed from months of experience here and at home with Mother. I plastered together two pieces of toast, each holding ninety-calorie pats of peanut butter, folded the bread into quarters, and flattened the slices into a pancake. I stuffed the toast into my underwear, where it would have to remain until I could figure out what to do with it. The blueberry muffin got squashed in my fist, and found a spot in the bony hollow under my left pelvis. (I did well forgoing my bikini panties for ample undies—every decision was marked by my singular and essential mission.)

When a staff nurse looked into my room and asked, "How are you doing?" I chewed on a fictional piece of fruit and nodded. "Fine," I grinned, and she was gone.

The sixty-five-calorie apple juice could be hidden in the bedpan disguised as pee. I had done away with 390 calories already. After more clever camouflaging and concealing, I calculated that I'd knocked off 420. I ate and drank what remained on the tray. The taste of two-percent milk stuck to my tongue like glue. It contained 130 calories, five grams of fat, and 100 percent rage.

Nurse Personality returned after thirty minutes, took inventory, and made note of the rather surprising outcome. Her eyes scanned mine with a spark of suspicion and she pronounced: "Your snack will be served at 10:30." She picked up the tray and left, reminding me that I had to finish the can of Ensure before then. I fell back onto my bed, my belly full with food and the tortured feeling that I could've done better to get rid of more.

While on this imposed regime of "bed rest," however, I kept moving. I squeezed my buttocks and did leg lifts, then sit-ups, then push-ups. I refused to let the calories conquer me.

When the toast and muffin began to irritate my skin, I removed them discreetly. My palms were clammy and my heart raced as I wrapped the neglected breakfast in paper towels and stuffed it under my mattress. I was pleased to have worked up a sweat from the stress of my elaborate routine. I could safely deduct thirty-five calories due to exhaustion.

Later in the day, I heard voices in the hallway. Through the window in the door I saw Nurse Personality, two other staff nurses, and Dr Messer doing morning rounds. They lingered in the room of the patient opposite, Nancy. She was a brilliant and flamboyant woman who suffered from, well, brilliance and flamboyance. I couldn't figure out why exactly she was here, what mental condition she had. Nancy was a forty-something lady who seemed chatty and highly educated and could switch quickly from masterful communicator to naïve child to oversexed tramp. She was a walking, living contradiction, as perhaps I was, although for different reasons. She'd been on the ward for several years. I began to worry that I would turn into her, if I stayed here long enough.

A curt knock on my door was followed by Dr Messer and his entourage. "Good morning," the doctor said. He was an elfish man, taut and thick, with reddish skin and thinning hair on a large, shiny skull that he would pat down with a sweaty handkerchief.

Although he was no taller than me, I always had the impression of looking up at him. Or was it because he was looking down at me? He had a way of walking across the room while I talked, his unblinking eyes pinned on me, as if he were mining my thoughts while scrutinizing my every gesture. Then he would stop, stare out the window, deliver a monologue conjured from my own outpourings, and having had the last word, swiftly stride out of the room.

"So? How does it feel to be eighteen?" He stood upright and tense, with his hands in his pockets. I turned away, avoiding his look, trying not to blast him with a sarcastic reply or break down in tears.

"I just turned eighteen yesterday."

"Yes, of course." He took a measured step, looking to the floor. "Well, maybe I'll ask you in a few days' time. You will probably know better then, I suppose?" He raised his head. Immediately his tone became serious. "Why did you run away? What exactly were you running away from?"

"From you. From this place. I can't stand it here!" I trembled and stared at everyone in the room.

"You mean you can't stand yourself."

"I didn't say that. You did."

"Two-hundred and ten," he said. "Do you know what that is?"

I sighed, not knowing where he was going with this. "Three thousand," I replied. "You know what *that* is? You doubled my calories without even telling me! How do you expect me to eat all that!" The food inside me curdled in a knot of torment.

He didn't flinch. "It's been 210 days. That's seven months, Lila. You've been in hospital for more than half a year. That's how long we've been keeping you alive." He poked his stubby finger into my collar bone. "You ran away because *you* can't stand *yourself.*"

I felt his breath on my face but said nothing. I wouldn't give him either an angry punchline or a helpless sob of submission.

"Think about it," he said. "You certainly have the time."

For the rest of the day, I remained numb in my dull, lifeless cell and opened my mind to the truth: Dr Messer failed to understand that the nature of my problem was not simply weight, calories, or fat. Nor was the problem me, for that matter. It was nature itself, and I would not be defenceless to its power. If I submitted to nature, then what remained? What would I return to? Who would I become?

Just when I thought it was gone for good, the pain from my injection had returned mysteriously, triggered, perhaps, by my family, who had come to visit me in hospital.

My father silently paced across the room with hands clasped behind his back, while my mother stared at me intently. "What are you doing to me, Lila? Don't you want to get well?" she asked. Her eyes appeared sleepless and weary.

All I could say was, "I'm sorry, Mother," although I knew I would do it all over again. How could I console her? My mother's face had changed since I'd been admitted. It had become gaunt and crumpled. Her relentless eyes searched mine for a glimmer of promise that I would be okay—that I *wanted* to be okay. Her hands reached for my skeletal limbs, pressing and massaging them, as if she were trying to revive a dead body.

Mina was curled up on the vinyl chair in the corner, her feet tucked in, examining her cuticles in silence. My skinny little sister was hardly little or skinny any more. She had blossomed into a full-figured young lady of sixteen with drop-dead good looks, street and book smarts, and a will of steel.

When Mother beckoned her, Mina pried herself out of her chair. She stood over me, looking around the room and then at her hand.

"I brought you chocolate." Her eyes widened. "Just kidding!" she said as a tear welled up. She rubbed it away. She tucked a glimmering silver bracelet into my fist, saying, "Happy birthday, fatso." Mina forced a smile, then covered her face with both hands and sobbed.

I lay there silently, a cold corpse, numb to her love. Where had I gone? Who had I become?

Mina wiped her face and looked at me, hurt by my lack of emotion, then covered it quickly with a tense smile. "C'mon, make a stupid wish."

I closed my eyes and wished I was dead.

I had been asleep for hours. In the dim room, my irises slowly opened up to take in the strange, murky yellow walls and shaded windows that overlooked the inner courtyard. Two cans of Ensure, 500 calories, and a plastic cup sat on my bedside table. I turned away.

My eyes landed on the tray table where a box wrapped in glittering baby-blue paper lay. I propped myself onto my elbows and squinted to put it into focus. It was my birthday gift from Dad.

My heart started to race. I threw off the blanket, placed my feet on the cold floor, and shuffled over to the tray table, arms outstretched, fingers reaching for the treasure. I held the package and felt its weight in my hungry hands. Then I slowly peeled the paper from the box and pried it open. Inside sat the handsome shiny body of a new camera. A real professional camera.

With a jerk, I raised it to my face, and pointed it out the window. Twisting my body from side to side, I saw only sooty darkness and the beams of light from rectangular windows across the courtyard. Patients wandered in and out of my view like walking ghosts. A milky-haired man planted himself at his window and stood there. He looked straight at me. Did he feel my camera on him? Did he know we had a bond because of this 50mm lens? I brought the camera down from my face and felt again its weight in the palm of my hand. The old man was no longer in the window. The window was gone. All lights were out.

Part Two:

Nymph

03. What Big Teeth You Have

My first ache for a sylphlike silhouette began in kindergarten, with Susan. Sweet, svelte Susan.

Mother dragged her reluctant six-year-old from her treasured second-hand Barbie doll house to St. Elizabeth Catholic school. There her stubborn daughter clung to her mother's pants and yelped out the names of imaginary guardian faeries who might rescue her from a life sentence of formal education. It was my first miserable day at school.

Horribly embarrassed, Mother chuckled and explained to the kindergarten teacher, Ms Rosemary, that I was cranky because I had not slept much the night before. I looked up at Ms Rosemary. She wore a turtleneck sweater that hugged her torso and was tucked neatly into her pencil-thin skirt, which carefully covered her kneecaps and exposed pale calves. With a crooked smile, she stood looking at me over her sharp nose. "Well, what a lovely, little … thing."

Ms Rosemary plucked me from Mother's thighs and planted me in the centre of the room, where I froze in silence as all eyes fell upon me. Mother took this opportunity to slip out.

I looked around at the blue-eyed, fair-haired children and realized that I was the only coloured kid in the room. A freckled boy with a thick body marched over, stood before me, and stared. I jerked my head back as he did a once-over and then pressed his hand on my forearm, rubbing it as if he were removing a stain.

"She's not dirty, she's just chocolate!" he yelled. "Yummy, I love chocolate!" I pulled my arm away just as his teeth were about to chomp into my flesh.

Girls shoved him away and gathered around me, fussing and giggling. Then the other boys joined them and they all flitted around me, but soon got distracted playing and crying, making friends and enemies, being girls and boys, naughty and nice.

It quickly became apparent to me that some children were more special than others. Like Susan, who was *not* made of chocolate. She was made of pure, charming cream. She had a luminous porcelain complexion, fine bones, and bird-like features. I had seen this girl in my fairy tale books. She and I were two of a kind, except that her feline beauty and slender figure seemed to reflect upon me like a ghastly shadow. Her light made me dark, darker than cocoa, blacker than midnight. I longed for her reflection to be mine and for my limbs to be lean like hers.

One afternoon, I decided to veer away from Susan's shadow and cast my own light. My singular feature, I knew, was not my skin or bones, but my thick, long dark hair. No other child in my class had hair as long, thick, and glossy as mine, and some of the girls had complimented me on it. Each morning, Mother braided it into two taut and sturdy ropes, but I longed to let my tresses loose, just as I had with the shiny and indestructible synthetic hair of my lovely blonde dolls.

While Ms Rosemary read to us from *Little Red Riding Hood*, my nimble fingers released the pinching rubber band, and I began to loosen my hair from the tip of the braid to the nape of my neck. I loved the feel of my hair skittering through my little fingers while Little Red Riding Hood went on her way through the forest. It was a strange and erotic sensation I had no language for, but it seemed as inevitable and as natural as my own breath. As Little Red Riding Hood met her grandma, my hair waterfalled down over my shoulders and plump, soft body. There I gleamed, alone in an imaginary spotlight.

"'Oh my, what big teeth you have, Grandma,' said Little Red Riding Hood," Ms Rosemary read.

"Oh look, Ms Rosemary! She's loosed up her hair!" chirped a little classmate.

Ms Rosemary looked sternly at me. "Lila! What are you doing? Look what you've done to your hair!" she chided.

The hungry wolf gobbled up Little Red Riding Hood and swallowed her whole. My hair hung suddenly like a wet mop. The spell was broken, the light extinguished, a shadow cast. I ballooned and my confidence was shattered, while Susan remained cool and slim as a porcelain figurine, perfectly intact.

I went home sobbing and angry. But that day, even my Barbie doll was no refuge. I noticed the unyielding physique of my doll. Like Susan and my pretty skinny sister Mina, Barbie's perfect, slim-waisted figure must have cast a spell on me. I plunged into playtime, at first pretending to be a princess and then a faerie, a winged creature. Wearing Mother's scarves, I acted out fantastic scenes and magical journeys to make up for that precious moment in the spotlight that had left me in shame. I was summoning a mythical being, a creature of boundless strength and beauty. Not quite human, she was slender and translucent. She would grow inside me and become stronger over time. This creature did not yet have a name.

My actual name was my only badge of pride. Lilting on the lips, melodic and glamourous, Lila was light. Lila was lithe. Lila was the sonorous expression of me, a name that gave me a reason to live up to it.

04. Grande Dame Madame Nature

When I turned eleven, time sped up. "Your menses have come early," Mother said, looking solemnly at my crimson-stained panties as though she were reading an obituary. She peered into the hallway, looked both ways, and led me by the hand from my bedroom into the bathroom. She locked the door. Then, unprepared and nervous, she initiated me into the rituals of feminine hygiene.

She bent down, opened a cupboard, and produced a big blue box. She set it down and looked at me while tapping the box. "*This* is what you use for *that*," she said, and showed me how to use a sanitary napkin, depressingly called "Always," and how to dispose of it: with discretion. She instructed me how to meticulously wrap the used napkin with endless rolls of toilet paper, hiding the *that*.

Her instruction complete, she patted me on the head, looked into my eyes, and said, "I'll buy you plenty of underwear."

I was devastated as much from the still unexplained bleeding as by her reaction to it. I didn't leave the bathroom for another hour, but stood with my back to the mirror, gazing numbly through eyes blurred by marble-sized tears. My childhood had been blown out of the water. This was when Monika rescued me.

My cousin Monika was my absolute idol. She had come to live with us a year earlier, after her parents had been killed in a car accident. Naturally, my father took in the daughter of his brother and became a parent to this parentless girl.

The day she arrived to live with us was a foggy Saturday morning in September, and there was a damp chill in the air. I had been guzzling the morning line-up of cartoons on television when I heard Dad's car pull up in the driveway. Immediately I shot up and went to the window, my heart racing wildly.

Dad got out of the Chrysler, opened the trunk, and pulled out several enormous suitcases. Monika emerged from the passenger seat, lifting herself out of the car with great effort. She was gripping the strap of an ochre satchel with both hands. Her raven-black hair fell onto her shoulders and folded into soft, perfect curls. Her eyes were cast down, but when she looked up and met my eyes, her face seemed to bloom like a flower.

She came into the house and took me in her arms. Her perfume and silky touch enveloped me, and in that instant I wished so much to be like her, to be able to live in my skin as she could.

I called her Moni. She loved the sound of that because to this material girl, it sounded like money, and she liked money. She liked the pleasures offered by popular culture: designer clothes, shopping sprees, malls and salons, sales and nails, big hair and *Marie Claire*. The glittery promises of advertising were her religion, and she believed with devout conviction all that was promised to her in cosmetic ads and advice columns. Her dresser was an altar, a shrine to beauty. We spent the entire day setting up her room, indulging in stories, and sharing secrets. She pampered me, brushed my hair, painted my fingernails, and made me her private doll.

When Monika found me crying the day I got my period, she took me to the mall to cheer me up. It was as if the glimmering store windows had been enchanted just for me. Holding my hand, we wandered through the bustling crowds and with the oddest mix of sweetness and sensibility, she educated me on the biological facts and functions of the inscrutable, enigmatic female body and demystified its mysteries. Big cousin informed little cousin that nature was simply taking its course. My body was just doing its job for grand dame Madame Nature. Moni had also gotten her period early, weeks after her tenth birthday, and had been thrilled about it.

At age sixteen, Monika inhabited her body as water inhabits a river. She was no knobby-kneed waif from a fashion magazine. She stood confident in her full female form and looked forward to her future.

What she had, I wanted for myself. The truth was, I felt in the marrow of my being that I was different. I was a fragile creature with a yearning to feel safe and loved; I could break under the slightest blow of rejection. Perhaps this fragility was another of my mother's genes that I had unwillingly inherited. She had already passed on to me her precious fat gene. Mother grew up in India, where plump little girls were praised and prized, and their healthy, ample bodies promised a future of childbearing womanhood. She now filled her lonely days with frying pakoras and baking brownies. And for that reason, my mother was my enemy. She was not my body's friend. But she saw herself in me, and I wanted to hold up a different mirror. And in that mirror was Monika.

05. Twelve and Turning

When my clock struck twelve, the spell was broken. The reverberations resonated one afternoon in sixth grade. It was recess, and I skipped off the playing field and into the school yard where my droopy-eyed girlfriends stood, posing as on the cover of *Mademoiselle*, fully loaded, ready to launch. These girls didn't wait for clocks and candles, bells and biology. They dove into little womanhood equipped with rules and attitudes, fashion and accessories. But there I was in a Scooby Doo T-shirt, still wearing braids, with a shameless disregard for style do's and don'ts and a plump figure already past puberty.

"Time to get those puppies strapped in, don't ya think?" said one of the flat-chested girls. Her eyes widened as others nodded in tandem. "Your mom's heard of training bras?"

I looked down at my chest, shocked at how my breasts were sculpted by my shirt. Instinctively I caved inward, as though I could make my developing breasts disappear.

My classmate's question seemed to suggest a certain lack of sophistication on my mother's part about dressing a developing daughter in the developed world. Training bras were, after all, a western invention. They assumed my mother was stuck in the backward ways of the old country, where pubescent girls flopped around uninhibited, destined to turn into the haggard old women with flaccid breasts and nipples pointing straight to earth as seen in *National Geographic.*

Since Mina had her own growth spurt at the age of ten, even earlier than I had, she now sported the cleavage of a grown woman. I watched with horror as boys chased her, tugging at her bra and taunting her until she broke down in tears. Beyond a sisterly bond, Mina was an extension of me. What happened to her, happened to me, only more deeply and fiercely.

That year on sports day, Mina came home empty-handed. Her tall, sturdy physique that foreshadowed early puberty had given her an athletic advantage over the small insect-like creatures that ran around spitting, pranking, and executing their "boys will be boys" license. She outran, out-jumped, out-shot-put, and outshone all the boys and girls in her grade. Although she retreated sobbing into her room that day, she was back on her feet in hours, indulging in life's new pleasures and admitting herself into a future of girlish vanity involving hair, makeup, and boys. I witnessed her last and final year of glory.

The clock's reverberations continued to resonate steadily, its vibrations now affecting the daddy of this daddy's little girl. My dad had been my childhood hero. To others he was scary looking—tall with a frowsy full beard and stern piercing eyes. But when Mina and I were kids, we could turn the serious scholar into the Queen of England in a matter of minutes. We would sit him down, braid his beard, stick ribbons and bows onto his head, smear lipstick and rouge on his face, and force him to be English.

"Welcome to our humble home, your majesty," we would say, bowing in our frocks.

"Why, it is my absolute honour," he would reply, sitting upright, sipping from a miniature tea cup. "I say, I love tea, but I do indeed enjoy a stiff shot of brandy from time to time."

We had no clue what brandy was, but we'd laugh uncontrollably. He'd invent silly games and tell us scary fairy tales. His universe of make-believe was well-suited to his dreamy-eyed faerie daughter.

But in my twelfth year, my father began to drift away from me, like a seaman journeying to another shore. Many evenings I would linger near him, bobbing up like a mermaid gasping for attention, but daddy's little girl was no longer little. Had I been a boy, would he have welcomed the maturing contours of my face and the developing shape of my body? Had I been a boy, would he have found in his growing son an impression of himself? Had I been a boy, would he have lowered his eyes when he saw me and turned away from physical affection? I could not be sure. But I was a girl. A girl who was growing up on him.

Mere months after my twelfth birthday, I began to experience strange sensations that made my hair stand on end and my skin flush. Mother Nature's love doctor, who was looking to amuse himself, had injected a hefty dose of the horny hormone into my arteries and put me under the spell of the once loathsome creatures: b-o-y-s.

It surged the summer our family camped in New Brunswick near Magnetic Hill, a landmark where cars defied gravity and rolled uphill. The sign posted at the souvenir shop read, "Magnetic or Magic?" My question exactly. My biology was consumed with boyology, and my mind had no influence over the chemical operations taking place in my body. My endocrine was in control, the rush of desire so complete it could not be matched any show of intelligence.

On our first day at the campsite, I sat down for breakfast at the picnic table and was suddenly jarred awake by the boys from the neighbouring campsite who were preparing for their morning swim. They paraded around in snug shorts, exposing their shiny, muscled torsos. My face felt hot with embarrassment as I munched on Corn Pops, nervously jerking my spoon through the clumpy powdered milk and gritty sugar. The most exceptional part of breakfast did not happen on the table but underneath it, where my naked thighs trembled and created their own magnetic magic.

Inevitably, I drifted toward the boys at the beach after breakfast. I sat in the shade of a dry branch and timidly hid my plump figure in a cocoon of discount beach towels in Miss Piggy pink, taking in the remarkable spectacle of boys being boys. I registered the scene in my mind's sensitive photographic film and slid the negative onto the evocative screen where dreams arose and where the bolt of reality could not reach. I was a lithe and honey-hued starlet, sprawled in her scarlet bikini, basking in the gloriousness of her own sun-shot beauty, and captivating the gaze of every handsome man—all of whom had cameras. Flash! "Who is the beautiful creature?" Flash! "So lovely, so fine. What's your name, darling?"

Of course, I shooed them away. "Oh please, it's too much! Leave me alone at once! No cameras!" But plump brown pubescent girls couldn't possibly be permitted such attention, let alone pleasure.

"Hey, weirdo," a voice said. Suddenly, sand grains stung my eyes. Through the searing sunlight, I saw the boys running away, laughing at me. The objects of my desire had dodged my daydream and turned it into a nightmare. They disappeared amid a trail of taunts and insults specially scripted for me. I was suddenly alone on the sand in my piggy-pink towel.

Was I a pervert? I asked myself. Were only the beautiful allowed to desire? Lurking underneath my questions was the brooding feeling that my sexual longing was perverse and could have fatal consequences. Didn't the fallen woman fall because her crime was to submit to lust? Wasn't feminine virtue virtuous because it symbolized victory over the primitive force of nature? And who was closer to nature than a lonely, hormonal girl of twelve?

06. Photographic Solution

My thirteenth year was spent far from home and in a hotbed of cultural confusion. And worst of all, I was away from Monika, away from our bond of belonging and my seeds of self-discovery. Did she know how miserable and lost I would be without her?

My father took us to India, where his family lived, for his sabbatical year. He handed his precious Leica to his gloomy daughter—"Here, use it to take pictures"—as though it could repair the rupture that he could see was tearing me apart. I hung the camera around my neck and wandered about, unable to capture the force and speed at which my new reality was penetrating my senses. It made me more anxious, so I put it away.

My accent and clothes gave me away as an outsider, a western girl. And all western girls were thought of as Lolitas. A wardrobe switch, however, would turn Lolita off and good Indian girl on.

On a sweltering hot August day, the marketplace was coming alive with vendors setting up their carts along the street. The hallucinating aromas of spices and succulent mangos saturated the muggy air. My grandmother had put some rupees in my purse so I could buy vegetables and fruit, with enough money left over for a treat. In my mind, I envisioned finding an object of vanity, some glass bracelets in bright pink or gold. "This is what Monika would get," I told myself. In her absence, I assumed the role of my idol. This is how I carried her inside myself.

Having applied a sheen of lip gloss and rouge, off I went. The excitement of going alone made me dizzy with happiness. My loose Indian *salwar* top was cool, more so because I had decided not to wear my camisole and the *dupatta*, a veil women wear that is part fashion accessory, part concealment, that covers the bosom.

As I strode across the street toward the market, I was struck by the crowds of men and boys. Their eyes penetrated me and seemed to fondle me in private places. Then, with a jolting shock, a stranger's hand grabbed my breast. My child brain did not, could not, at first, register what was happening. Then our eyes locked. The man's face glistened with sweat, his eyes were bloodshot, and a broad moustache stretched over a sinister grin. His foul scent seeped into my brain. Click. In extreme close-up, filling the frame of my inner eye. I jerked away, and the stranger was lost among the bodies—never to be seen again, but never to be forgotten.

I returned to my grandmother's house empty-handed. Mother discovered me sobbing in my room, and seeing my camisole and *dupatta* thrown over the chair, instructed me never to leave the house again without wearing them. I wanted desperately to erase the picture impressed on my mind's eye, to camouflage the foul scent that had entered my pores, the grotesque sensation of his sweaty palm pressing into me. Over many nights, I fantasized my revenge, but I was always left with the nagging feeling that I had only myself to blame.

For the next several weeks, I hardly left the house. Then I had the impulse to pick up my father's Leica. Its cool metallic body glistened against the dusty gold light of late evening, and the smooth glassy lens winked as if to welcome me into a substitute world. I carried my father's camera around my neck for the rest of my time in India. When I wasn't taking photos, it rested against my bosom like a shield. I pointed the lens at men who would assault me with their gestures and gazes and felt a sense of power and authority not usually granted to young girls.

Once my new hobby of intimidation had cooled my burning anger, I found something more deeply satisfying about photography. I saw through the lens what was invisible to the naked eye. The box contained a secluded universe that I could disappear into and be witness to a remarkable world that choreographed light, perspective, and form and refracted reality into a delectable dream. I could capture time and fix it with a single click of the shutter.

Then something incredible began to happen. The first pulsations of a creature were being born inside me, pushing against my skin, and emerging into some enchanted thing. It began to take shape in my consciousness; it was on its way to becoming almost real. I secretly called her "Faerie."

Back at home in Quebec, my father's camera remained a necessary appendage. I loved the images that I captured, filling the gaping spaces in my heart, frame by frame. I plastered my room with my photographs, scenes and moments that had slipped through the cracks of reality and the immediacy of sensations.

And I was no longer interested in the bodies of boys and men or in the images of gorgeous pop stars and sexy movie idols. No erotic desire blazed inside me. I wondered if this was due to the workings of the faerie creature inside me.

Since our return from India, Monika spent most evenings sulking at the dinner table. Worse, she usually kept her bedroom door closed; I was no longer welcome in her room to play and witness her daily beauty rituals. When she did find me messing with her *maquillage*, she screamed at me, "Get the hell out, you pest!" She and Dad argued almost every day, especially when she came home late. She was standing up to my father in ways I would never dare. My mother did not intervene. Her role was to defuse the situation with food.

I listened to the heated exchanges between Monika and Dad through the bedroom wall, biting my cuticles until they bled. Our happy home movie had turned into dreadful documentary, a real-life horror of clashing wills as I watched the perfect image of my idealized grownup self coming undone.

In a few months time, Monika would be gone, her room vacated, and her memory buried like a distant dream.

07. Hit of Numbers and Nature

At age thirteen, Mina was a faithful subscriber to *Seventeen* and followed its exhaustive beauty advice to the letter, from cuticle care to the painstaking treatment of teenage acne.

Meanwhile, my morning routine was just insane. Every morning I took on the weigh scale with the fury of a boxer facing her opponent. I stepped on the scale and braced myself for the punch: 1-2-1. I stepped off in shock, unable to fathom that I'd gained weight while on a slimming diet. I looked at my bloated brown figure in the mirror, my deceiving double. My instinct was to turn away, but I looked hard and long. I hadn't done that since I was twelve, when the shock of pubic hair and sudden bulge of breasts sent me into a tailspin of suicidal grief. Two years on, the grief was intensifying.

In a daze, I stepped into the tub and ran hot water over my head and down my back, utterly disappointed with myself and my disobedient body. My breasts and belly extended into a grotesque shape. A handful of flesh on my belly had ballooned over my panty line, my thick upper thighs pressed tightly against one another, and my face was full and round, the hollow of cheekbone lost under flab. No space. No bone. No self-control. I longed for jutting pelvic bones and a glorious thigh gap, for a sunken inward-curving abdomen under a visible ribcage. Like the cover model of *Elle*, whose light figure floated on the glossy page in her two-piece and carefree sheen.

I stepped into my stiff jeans and tugged them over my legs and thighs. I had gained a whole size. If that wasn't punishment enough for my deplorable lack of discipline, I had to expose this body to the world and, worse, to my grade-nine classmates. It was gym day.

By the curious and cruel hand of fate, I was surrounded in my small-town Catholic school by beautiful tall girlazons, all fed on the same diet of pop culture. While they were faithful followers of fashion and celebrity trends, I was subject to the discount and hand-me-down ethos of my mother, a leftover of her early years as an immigrant. Mother was a faithful fan of the "marts" of Quebec: Bonimart, K-Mart and, her favourite, Miracle Mart. Unfortunately for me, the cult of the marts had resulted in a tacky wardrobe of styles and colours well-suited for Halloween, not for high school.

In my hideous gym shorts, I braced myself for a snide remark about my unshaven ape legs from the boys whose own fur would never meet the cruel sting of a razor or a humiliating remark. I had once heard that the hair of Punjabi girls was thicker, darker, and more tenacious than that of white girls, and that no amount of shaving, waxing, or grooming could conquer the mighty Punjabi follicle. I don't know if this was true, but I figured that I was living proof. While Mina had inherited my mother's hairless gene, I had—just my luck—inherited the hairy gene of auntie Gurinder Kaur from Patiala, well-known for her spectacular furry unibrow.

"Today we're outside," said Mr Reed, our phys-ed teacher,

pointing his stubby finger toward the doors. We hauled ourselves off the benches and into the crisp, frigid air. The shock of cold pleased me. I was glad to be outdoors, where I was liberated from thinking, and my body was free to experience the mechanical grind of physical activity. I ran across the soggy field and icy grass. Fuelled with fat, my thighs thundered as each foot landed on the ground. As I orbited the track, I heard Mr Reed barking, "Ladies, move your fat butts!" provoking the boys to push back against any traces of femininity in themselves, as if it were a disease, and impelling the girls to loathe our own natures. I ran, fuelled by those words, and set in motion the faerie creature, who followed the laws of a different nature, one not ruled by sex or size, age or time.

08. Don't Stand So Close to Me

I began to keep a daily log of my caloric intake after reading an article in Mother's most recent issue of *Good Housekeeping*. It said that "diets were impractical without a calorie diary" and offered a list of helpful tips to curb carb cravings. It also gave suggestions of low-calorie alternatives: "Craving chocolate? Have a stick of celery. Hankering for a hamburger? Nibble on cucumber." As a bonus, the magazine included a complimentary calorie counter.

I found the perfect calorie diary in my dad's university office one afternoon while I waited for his Friday lecture to end. It was a crimson notebook with a glossy cover that beckoned me like an Eden-red apple. Inside, it was blank, with smooth, pure white pages lined with grids—pages upon pages of miniature squares into which I could scribble a single caloric digit. The fixed and definite lines were comforting; they reassured me that my goal was at hand. There was no room to wander, to digress with words and wants and feelings.

This time, I told myself, I'm really going to get the weight off. I will be methodical about jotting down every morsel, every crumb, anything short of my own saliva. My mission was to be more disciplined, and this diary would be my first symbolic gesture.

1 whole wheat toast = 72 calories
250 mL 2% milk = 120 calories
1 tbsp strawberry jam = 15 calories

Glorious! I was excited to find a new tool, and one small enough to keep in a deep secret pocket.

Not like my other diary, which was bulky and bloated with outpourings of grief, scribblings of heartache and disenchantment, of brooding and longing. Lots of longing. If longing were food, it would be a calorie-busting serving of English fish and chips. Notes from my grade-ten diary:

I have fallen headfirst for my English teacher. He looks like he just walked out of a music video. More precisely, he looks like "Don't Stand So Close to Me" Sting. This underaged girleen is getting herself into some double deep trouble.

Let me recall the delicious moment when I first laid my eyes on dreamy Mr Black. It was a dull Monday early in November, when red poppies appear pinned on collars and suits and forgotten old soldiers turn up on street corners, only to fade out again until the following November. The opiate poppy seemed to have produced in me the dreamiest feeling as I sleepwalked from the school bus into the classroom and saw him standing near his desk in a streak of sunshine. He turned to look at me just as I saw him, and in that moment our eyes locked. It was as though he had emerged from the belly of an ancient dream to appear before me. My gaze fell to my feet, and I folded myself into my dependable desk. How does one respond to the first shivering moment of desire?

There was a commotion in the classroom, hissing, whispers, coughing chuckles. Curious glances and notes were exchanged across the rows of desks.

"Morning!" The room stilled as the teacher picked up a dusty stick of chalk and produced his name on the board with the force of a swordsman.

"I am Mr Black. Andrew Black." He put down the chalk, slapped the magic powder from his princely palms, and swept his gaze across the alert row of teens, skirting the starry-eyed girl in the third row who was inwardly serenading him already. He was, he said, our newly hired English teacher.

His words melted into a watery mumble in my ears as he told us that he had travelled from his native England to the US, and his desire to learn French had led him north to Quebec, where ironically, he was teaching English. As he spoke, my alert senses captured his handsomeness. He was over six feet tall and wore a tweed jacket with the dishevelled swagger of a rock star. My Sting substitute made generous use of his hands. He expressed himself well, ending statements with a sweep of his fingers through his fair hair. His pale skin produced a nutty scent of talcum powder and almond, which evaporated over the hours and became a sort of accidental barometer of the time of day.

"What brings me here, dear students, is literature." He stopped less than a foot away from my desk. I slowly, cautiously looked up at him, and he met my gaze. A beat short of drawing attention to his singular deliberation of me, he tapped my desk lightly, as if to produce a mental *nota bene* from this arrested moment, and carried on with his introduction.

For the remainder of the class and for the rest of the week, he paid me no attention. I longed for another flaming spark to set me ablaze, but each time I passed him in the hallway or class-room, he carried on in the ordinary guise of a regular teacher. After three weeks, I assumed that my face had blended into his mental blur of all the girls' faces—if it had ever existed for him at all. I surrendered to the realization that my infatuation was spurred on by my own loneliness and self-loathing, and that it never could have had any reciprocal power.

One day, I'd just eaten the banana bread planted in my lunch box by Mother. I ate it because it was there. I ate everything, even when I felt full. *Fat, thoughtless cow*, I said to myself.

After lunch, I shut my lonely 126-pound self in a bathroom stall in the girls' washroom. I fell to my knees, and with a ball of toilet paper, soaked up my baboon tears. In this private confessional, I admitted my weaknesses to an unseen witness. I listed in my mind numerous infractions and transgressions, the calories and desserts, the despicable deluge of desire, my immense appetite for love, and for that horrid banana bread. Consumed with guilt and a gut-wrenching hunger for more, I could feel my belly swelling up and the flooding feeling rising in disgust. It reached my esophagus and rose into the back of my throat. Suddenly, a wellspring of all the sin gushed out fully, completely evacuating my body.

I was pure again. I was absolved. Immediately I experienced

a sense of bliss, an intoxicating rush of power from my empty stomach. My throat felt hot, and the veins in my temples throbbed. I curled over the toilet bowl and saw through moist eyes a blur of brownish-yellow vomit. The vile odour rose to my nostrils, jolting me into a recognition of what I had done. There it was. It had a form, colour, and smell. The shape of how I felt. I wiped my hot face and acrid lips with toilet paper and flushed the toilet. I watched the bowl fill up again, dutifully rising with a pool of clear water. Clean and renewed.

Mr Black walked toward us and addressed me directly. "Hello. Lila, is it?"

The girls standing in the hall turned their heads to look at me. I pretended that I hardly noticed him and looked sideways, toying with my school bag zipper.

"Yeah," I said breezily. Surprisingly, the girls didn't seem to notice how strangely I was behaving and how wildly I wanted him.

"She has a weird name," Christine blurted out.

"It is not!" I gave her a cutting look and told Mr Black that I was named after my maternal grandmother, conjuring up a fictional melodrama from the workings of my brain's imagination, then realized how dull it was when I saw him blink, I feared, out of boredom.

He interjected in a low cottony voice. "Lila is a mythical name, short for Delilah in Hebrew." My heart stopped and my limbs became weak. Had he just compared me to the infamous temptress?

"To us, it means lollipop!" The girls giggled, then turned quiet when Mr Black gave them a dour look.

"If you girls are as clever as you think you are, then I expect ingenious papers on your next assignment. Christine will have the privilege of reading hers first," he said with a cheeky grin. He grazed my arm with his hand as he brushed past me, saying, "See you ladies then. Ta-ta."

As I entered the classroom, Mr Black called me to his desk. I froze for a moment, then felt myself involuntarily floating toward him. He slid my graded paper toward me. "Fine work, Lila," he said, and I saw the spiked thrust of an A+. "I would like you to read your story to the class. It provides an excellent example of tragedy and internal conflict in character." I nodded stiffly. The perspective from the front of the class was jarring, but I had no time to get comfortable with the faces and eyes directed at me. I fumbled with my paper. Once I got through the first paragraph, however, I became remarkably calm, and the sentences began to flow off my tongue. When I was done, some of the girls made snide comments, but Mr Black hushed the class and praised me for my imagination and creative writing style. Instantly, his words erased the remarks from my peers.

Soon after, I began to outdo myself with each new paper, story, and essay for English class. But I neglected my duty to my calorie diary, filling the pages with a troubling number of flowers, floating hearts, winged butterflies, squiggly designs, and incomprehensible scribblings.

One winter afternoon after school, while waiting for the bus with Mina, I realized that I had forgotten my pencil case in the classroom. I hurried back and saw my crinkly Little Mermaid case where I had left it on my desk. When I turned to leave, Mr Black was standing before the blackboard looking at me. Behind him, the empty blackboard was filled with ghost words that wriggled out of recognition and floated into my memory of past lessons.

"Forgot this," I said with a crooked smirk and showed him my pencil case.

"Lila, hang on a second, please," he said. I stopped at the door and held my breath. This was the first time I had been alone with him—outside of delusional fantasies knit together from Hollywood romances and subtitled Bollywood fare.

"May I ask you something?" He took a few slow steps toward me. During that pregnant pause, I imagined him uttering everything from commenting about my writing to proposing marriage.

"What do you think, Lila, of a drama club?"

"What do you mean?" I gulped.

"How would you and your classmates like to set one up?"

"That's not exactly a bad idea," I said.

He beamed at me. "Good, we shall set one up then." He then winked and turned to carry on with whatever he'd been doing before I walked in, as though I were no longer there. My heart sank, struck by how curtly I could be dismissed. But I couldn't get myself to tell him that I had missed my bus, let alone ask to use his phone to call Dad. Instead, I lingered like a lost kitten.

He turned and looked at me. "Oh dear. You missed your bus, didn't you? I am so sorry, Lila. If you'd like, I could give you a lift home." How quickly the heart bounces back!

As he drove, I took in the scent of his sleek silver Volvo, which smelled like sage and pine and the cultured smell of Europe. I was transported into a foreign universe where we were lovers, driving along sinewy roads in the Alps toward a glorious mountain lodge where he would light a blazing fire and feed me champagne and strawberries.

"I've yet to try maple syrup. I hear it's sweeter than sugar," he said. He had been talking about foods he hadn't sampled yet since moving to Quebec.

I concurred and said, "I'd like to try caviar. Have you ever had caviar?" I exhaled my (imaginary) Virginia Slims through the window into the alpine air as we drove past Neuschwanstein, the German castle I pictured looming beyond the Swiss Chalet diner ahead of us.

"Why on earth would a girl your age want to try fish eggs?"

"What would you know about 'a girl my age'? A girl my age likes a lot of things." I turned to him. "I *have* been to Europe, you know."

He looked at me with a smirk. "I'm sure you have. Trust me, a *girl your age* would not like caviar!"

I fell into a silent tantrum and sat tight-lipped and pouting for a long juvenile while. Lover had turned into disapproving parent, snatching the cigarette from my lips and tossing it out of my daydream.

"I am *not* a kid," I finally said.

"I can see that. You're a lovely young lady." He turned and looked at me with the eyes of an onscreen lover. His gaze lingered on me, then travelled south. How much of this was my imagination and how much was real, I wondered. I felt a mix of arousal and repulsion that now coalesced into fear. I was a kid. I wanted to be a kid. I was ready to try new things, yes, but sex? That was still something reserved for big-bodied, adult mammals. Also, what did I know about Mr Black, really? His life was in shadow. Who was he? Did he have a girlfriend, a wife, an ex-wife? A fiancée, perhaps?

"Turn over there," I said, relieved to see the blinking Dairy Queen sign with its familiar frosty white cone welcoming me home. As he pulled up to my doorstep, he turned to me and smiled vaguely, wishing me a fine weekend. Before I shut the door, he added, "Apologize to your parents for me for having made you miss your bus."

I nodded, then watched him pull away. He seemed so dull and perfunctory, but it occurred to me that he was trying to restore the official bonds that fell within the lines of the law. He was harnessing his desire and nudging his pupil back behind her desk.

In my bedroom, I saw my calorie diary tucked on the shelf and my heart sank. I opened it and resolutely put pen to paper, as if to restrain my unwieldy imagination and desire.

Ham sandwich = 230 calories (As I watched him in the
school yard.)

Bag of potato chips = 250 calories (When he caught me
staring at him.)

Chocolate brownie = 430 calories (The embarrassment his
look brought on.)

I put the caloric diary back on the shelf and lay on the bed,
head under my pillow.

Within weeks we had a drama club set up in an empty classroom. Mr Black assigned me the role of Juanita, a jaded Span-
ish mistress, probably because she and I shared the same tawny
racial shade and full figure. The scrawny white girls in the club
would play fair maidens who, unlike the temptress, were fated to
happy endings.

In rehearsal, Mr Black and I had our first real argument. According to the script, when Juanita, a poor farm girl, is dumped
by her married lover, she goes mad and spends the rest of her
days in an asylum. When I argued that losing her marbles over
a man who did not love her would not be true to her character,
Mr Black pointed out that this was not up for negotiation and
that, "the director's job is to carry out the vision of the writer, and
the actor's job is to carry out the vision of the director. Is that
clear?" I had been chastened and put in my place. Now when we
rehearsed, Mr Black remained cool and cordial, always curt. The
tender and warm timbre of his voice seemed to have vanished.

How had I become hideous to him so suddenly? Because I had stood up for myself as a grownup woman?

And I had literally grown—to an appalling 130 pounds. I was heavier than any girl in the class and possibly the school. I wanted to be loved more than I cared to be right. I wanted to run into his arms and submit so that he would speak sweetly to me again.

On the eve of the performance, I tried to rehearse my lines before the bathroom mirror, but my mind went blank. I began jumbling up my dialogue, reconfiguring it into utter nonsense. In sheer panic, I crept into the kitchen at midnight and sought comfort from a box of stale Girl Guide cookies that I had hidden in the shady underbelly of the pantry. In the freezer I discovered a hibernating carton of ice cream. I gorged myself in the dimly lit kitchen, with the steady hum of the refrigerator for company, seeking the anaesthetic bliss that food brings. In those precious minutes I existed in a private parenthesis of absence, a limitless curve splintered from real time and any semblance of bodily existence. Before long, I had consumed half of the box of cookies and left the ice cream container with just a few guilty spoonfuls of Rocky Road. Within moments, I felt a rush of panic and anxiety, and I began to feel sick. I ran to the bathroom and curled over the toilet, nudging my fingers down my throat, but I couldn't purge and undo the moment of weakness. I drank half a litre of water instead, lumbered back to my bedroom, and fell asleep.

The next day, we excitedly collected backstage and wrangled into our costumes. Mine was an azure skirt and embroidered shawl. At the tables where we put on our makeup, the big bright light-bulbs framed us, making everyone appear larger than life and gorgeously famous. My heart fluttered with pride at the magical illusion that transformed us scruffy, sweaty high school kids into stars. In my mirror, I accentuated my features with a smear of lipstick and stroke of eyeliner. How grownup I looked, my baby face chiselled with blush along an imaginary cheekbone. The woman in the mirror looked back at the young girl. Was she seeing my future?

A cheery voice brought me out of my reverie. "This is your day!" said Mr Black as he swam into the room in his sea-green shirt with hair combed back in a silky wave. "You all look splendid." I was swept away in his undertow, all my self-possession gone. Mr Black's spectacularly handsome image multiplied madly in the mirrors lining the walls of the room, making me dizzy. The rogue wave took me far from shore. I fumbled with makeup, a hairbrush, seaweed and sandy pebbles.

"Are you alright, Lila?" His eyes met mine in the mirror and I froze.

"I know I've been hard on you, but it doesn't mean that I don't care. I know that you'll be absolutely brilliant tonight."

I looked back at him with a trembling smile.

The play unfolded perfectly. Once the spotlight fell on my face and the warmth from the audience blanketed the stage, I slipped into character. The school year ended with roaring applause, and in sad, ecstatic silence, I whispered to myself, "Encore, encore."

09. Homecoming

During the lonesome summer that followed, dullness hung over me like a wet wool blanket. The thought of not seeing Mr Black for the entire summer only made matters worse. Not even my camera could tempt me out of my depression; it sat on the shelf like a relic, collecting dust.

"Go play outside!" Mother would yell when she caught me wandering through the dim hallways during the dull afternoons.

One day, as my thoughts drifted aimlessly as I hit a tennis ball against the side of the house, I heard a familiar, honeyed voice.

"Well? Aren't you going to say hello?"

I dropped my racket to my thigh. It was Monika. I hadn't seen her for so long, and now she seemed so different. Firm, sure-footed.

She walked up and embraced me. "Look at you! You're so grown up now, Lila."

The door burst open and Mother emerged, wiping her hands with a dishtowel, trailing a gust of acrid garlic from her Saturday cooking. She squinted at us, then gasped when she recognized Monika.

"I was in town, so I thought I'd drop by," Monika offered.

Mother lowered her face into her garlicky towel and sobbed with happiness.

In the living room, Mother served tea from a tray using our best china cups and a plate of Peak Freans, the kind with a red glob of jelly in the centre that made them look like Christmas tree decorations. This formality only seemed to make the reunion more tense. Small talk skipped between the unusually humid weather, the latest episodes of *Oprah*, and Indian celebrity gossip. Mother safely dodged the topic uppermost on our minds, but she hadn't stopped grinning. I observed her glow as she spoke to Monika, alternating between Punjabi and English, engaging in the hybrid tongue she usually only shared with Dad. Now she spoke to Monika as one adult *janani* to another. The room got hotter and the tea darkened as the afternoon wore on. Dad would soon walk through the door. Would his eyes fill with anger? Sadness? Or just restrained surprise?

It was a sweltering summer day when I had last seen Monika. I watched from my bedroom window as Dad paced back and forth on the front lawn, screaming at her. I had never witnessed Dad in such a rage. Within half an hour, Monika had packed and was swallowed into a cab and driven away from our home. Monika, the straight-A student, studious and hard-working, helpful at home, the perfect babysitter to her young cousins. A good girl. What had she done that had been so terrible? What shameful, hideous thing? She did what many children do to their parents: she deviated from his expectations of her. Six months before that front yard drama, Monika had announced to my dumbstruck parents that she was going to marry her lover.

"Who is this? Who is he—this, this 'lover' of yours?" my father demanded. Monika had told them that she was dating a man more than twice her age, a divorced truck driver from Shawinigan.

"How did you meet this man?" was his next question. She admitted that he'd given her a lift as she was hitchhiking alone one weekend night after a party. He wasn't just a truck driver, she insisted; he was an engineer.

Dad stared at her as though she was a stranger who had hijacked his niece. "Have you forgotten your heritage, your honour, and your duty to your family?" He reminded her that he and Mother had planned a different future for her: she was to get a university degree in pharmacology, then marry a professional—and a Punjabi boy. There was no other way.

Monika said she would not leave Jacques. The argument volleyed back and forth, but Monika reminded him that in a few days, when she turned eighteen, Dad would have no authority over her. So he gave her an ultimatum. If she left with this "Mr Lorry Driver," she would not be welcomed back. Despite her adult call to arms, Monika broke down in tears and agreed to break off the engagement. Everything seemed to return to almost "normal" for a few weeks.

We had just finished our usual Sunday lunch and Monika had gone outside to water the lawn when the phone rang. Mother answered and raised the receiver for Dad. He became unusually silent after taking the phone, and I turned to look at him. His expression went from a perplexed frown to fury.

"Attend what? I'm sorry, I am not following … What are you talking about? … Are you sure? No, she is not. This is impossible. There must be a mistake."

Without a goodbye, he hung up the phone and stared in shock. He said something quietly to Mother and headed down the hallway toward Monika's room, pushed open her door, and walked in. But Monika wasn't there.

She was in the garden hosing the rose bush. She wore a buttercup yellow T-shirt and denim shorts, and the misty water cast her in shimmering stardust. Dad stormed outside. "*Ki kitta tune? Sharam nahee andhi!*" he roared as he marched toward her and snatched the hose from her hand. A flurry of vexed Punjabi obscenities tumbled from his tongue. Monika tried to plead with him, but my educated, progressive, westernized father channelled the old-world convictions of past generations. Monika was his flesh and blood. He was, in his rage, immune to the influence of higher education, western ways, and modern life with its liberal leanings. Monika carried a responsibility, unique to the children of immigrants, to uphold the traditions and values of the land which had birthed her parents' generation while excelling with competitive rigour in the traditions of the host country. It was a delicate cultural balancing act, and Monika had failed.

Mr Lorry Driver's parents had phoned to invite us to celebrate the good news and were sorry we were out of the country and could not attend the wedding.

Once she left, we obeyed an unspoken rule that her name was not to be uttered. Dad transformed Monika's room into a library. The reconstruction of this room took up most of his time outside his academic and domestic duties. I helped him classify books, paint hard-to-reach corners, and accompanied him to furniture stores. I was ever the obedient little child. Never did I want to trigger in him the anger he felt for Monika. I would not dare to grow up on him now.

"*Aunty ji* ... " Monika lowered her voice. "He treats me well. He is a good husband." Then her manicured hand fell on her belly. "We're expecting ..." Mother brought her hand to her mouth as though covering her lips would hold back her tears. "I'm happy, *Aunty ji*. I want nothing but your blessing."

Monika walked over to my mother and, crouching down, folded her arms about Mother's broad ample figure.

We then heard the low rumble of Dad's Chrysler, the slam of the car door. Monika gave me a winking smile, as if to say that all would be okay. Mother stood up stiffly and walked into the kitchen. We heard whispers, then Dad appeared in the doorway. He looked first at me, then at Monika, who had risen to her feet.

"Hello, uncle."

He stared at her for a moment and, without a word, turned and disappeared down the hallway. We heard the library door shut with a resolute click.

Monika's shoulders slumped in resignation.

Mother let out a sigh. "He'll come around. Don't worry."

Monika gave me a feeble hug before leaving again, without my father's blessing.

By the end of that summer, I weighed 135 pounds.

10. The Heavy

The school yard clamoured with excited, bronzed teens who boasted about their summers and stood tall and gorgeous in their tall fashions. I stepped off the school bus and made my way to the classroom. I had graduated from juvenile backpack to senior shoulder bag, which held promising new notebooks awaiting lessons from him. My longing for Mr Black had grown exponentially during the endless solitude of my summer, especially after Monika had left again. I had been waiting to relive the precious moments when our eyes first locked.

When I looked in the classroom door, however, he was not where my fantasy needed him to be; instead, we found a dull substitute. Mr Black had been called back to England and would not be returning. I expected to be disappointed, but my immediate response was sweet relief. I was glad he was gone. And then I overheard gossip so incredible it left me breathless. Mr Black hadn't been called away; he'd been sent away because of a girl named Marie Namur, a mousy-haired grade-nine student. She'd exposed, in a detailed letter to the school, the unspeakable indiscretions of her private tutor, teacher, and mentor. When he was confronted with these allegations, he didn't deny them and was prepared to face the consequences of his actions. He was told to leave the school.

Thoughts of Marie tormented my dreams. We shape-shifted

and entered each other's bodies. Not one, but two Mr Andrew Blacks savagely penetrated us. My subconscious mind went crazy trying to seal the gap between the man I fantasized about and the monster he was. How could I have been consumed by passion and yearning for this man? My world began to split from the one in which I was living, separated by an imperceptible seam.

I tore out the soiled pages from my diary. Purified of all evidence of weakness and failure, lean with virgin pages and perfect white grids drawn with sleek blue lines, my calorie diary had been there all along. Faithful. Dependable. Unstoppable.

I separated my bloated toes over the filmy window and saw the needle tremor at my inhalation of hope, then settle on the 140 mark. I hopped off the bathroom scale and stared at the instrument in disbelief. I readjusted it, turning the sensitive dial back and forth, zeroing the needle perfectly, then stepped back on and held my breath, as though a pound or two would magically vanish from sucking air into my lungs. Air is air. Flesh is flesh. One hundred and forty pounds of it.

It was just weeks before graduation, and I had never been this heavy. I had never been so depressed. The logical solution? Lose weight. Get lighter. Feel better. Somewhere along the way, all other desires had fallen away. No longer was it important to be brainy or beautiful or fair. The pursuit of beauty was pedestrian, and having a fair complexion was as possible as growing a moustache; I could not make myself white any more than I could become a boy. I formed a single-minded obsession with my weight and a desperate need to arrest time itself. Because in time, I would be a grownup woman.

One hundred and forty was the heaviest I would allow myself to be. There would be less of me from here on. Less flesh. More time.

I slipped the dress over my up-stretched arms in the Bonimart fitting room, but it stopped at my 36D chest, and the puffy satin sleeves hung there, flapping over my face. There was no zipper or hook to release me and let the dress fall as it was meant to; the designer made this for a flat-chested girl and not a fully endowed female.

I faced the mirror. A pink blimp reflected back at me.

Mother tapped on the door. "So? How is it? Let me see."

"No!" I begged her. She came in anyway and scanned my figure. Her eyes brightened. "Lila, you look so beautiful. Like a fairy tale princess!"

On graduation day in the school auditorium, the graduates lined up, giddy for their moment of stardom and eager for their rolled-up, ribbon-tied prize. As I approached the stage, I kept repeating, like a prayer, "I want this to mean something. I want this to mean something." I had made the honour roll and had top marks in literature. For that I was proud. But pride was overshadowed by shame over the digits on the scale.

In the crowd of parents, I spotted the round brown face of my mother among the wash of white. Dad was positioned on the aisle with his new camera. My legs and arms quivered and trembled like jelly, but I moved forward involuntarily, an actress in a drama who seemed to have been wrongly cast. What was I graduating from? Or to?

We students were then ushered from the auditorium and out onto the lawn under the wide poplars and ancient oak trees. A lazy golden light cascaded over me as Dad positioned me for a picture. Click. My eyes blinked as the shutter did. Both the camera and I conspired to capture the truest expression of what that moment felt like: a very bad picture.

At the prom, the "ladies" were cupcake-coloured in frilly frocks while the "gentlemen" wore black tuxes. Bubbly in flute glasses was served to us as we entered Auberge La Comtesse, a restaurant known to host everything from proms to wedding receptions to the occasional wake. I was dateless, wearing a powder-blue chiffon dress that Mother had stitched from a design I'd quickly sketched, and I'd also bought my own corsage. Some of the other students probably thought it was sad, but I feigned a smug, superior attitude.

After the formal dinner and dance, most of us wound up in a basement at a house party. Immaturity inevitably cracked through the crust of sophistication as some of the kids indulged in spectacular binges of booze and pot. Inevitably, up-dos came undone, and lipstick got smeared across boys' cheeks. I sat quiet and dangerously sober on an orange beanbag chair, sipping diet soda. The faerie squirmed inside the translucent walls of her chrysalis.

A heavy foreboding made the summer heat worse. The jaws of September, two months away, would swallow me into the belly of an expectant, fruitful future. I packed away the scale, unable to face the digits that climbed despite weighing myself each day at exactly the same time and in the same way—necessarily naked, bowels empty, ravenously hungry, and angry at myself for not trying harder.

I distributed my résumé to clothing stores and fast food chains for a chance at my first summer job. The best I could come up with was cleaning the salad bar at a local restaurant, a better job than any faerie could hope for. I refilled the little baskets with chopped carrots and cabbage, wiped Thousand Island and oily French dressing off the counter, and polished off the smudges made by hungry customers on the sneeze guard. It was a simple, noble job, if mind-numbing, and it was my saving grace from the mental gymnastics I'd been performing since graduation. The hours of scheduled routine were a welcomed respite from myself.

After work, I'd meet Mina at the tennis court to play a few rounds until suppertime. From across the court I gazed at my little sister. Her white boy shorts sat on narrow hips, exposing her trim, dark-caramel midriff. A mango-green bandana stretched across her firm, full breasts. She sprang forward on the court with assurance and nimble athleticism and swung her racket from muscled brown shoulders, strong from summers spent swimming and winters shovelling. At fifteen, she was eager to part with childhood and experience the freedoms and pleasures of adulthood. I seemed only to become rounder, softer, sadder. We were bonded by blood but separated by nature.

Outside of the routine, I existed in a state of restlessness that I could not work off with a brisk jog or evening bike ride. When the feeling became unbearable, I retreated to my bed to contain my trembling limbs, like a pupa wound up in bedding. With a soft ripping sound, the skin of my cocoon tore as the faerie began her escape. Time slowed and the heavy would soon be light.

It was the Monday morning of the week before I was to start college. I awoke with a burning impulse to step on the scale. I didn't feel physically different, but something felt odd, as though I'd undergone an internal, molecular realignment. The needle settled on 112. I zeroed it obsessively, the musician tuning her precious instrument, but it was not off-key. Hidden in my billowy T-shirts and baggy trousers, I hadn't realized that I'd lost weight. Apart from a diligent duty to my calorie diary, I had made no deliberate effort to lose weight. Not even the daily rounds of tennis with Mina could account for this drastic weight loss. Nor had I abstained from Mother's Peak Freans. I could think of only one explanation: the persistent and petulant magic of melancholy, which burns more calories per hour than a workout or military drill, because unlike a rigorous thirty-minute cardio routine, it operates relentlessly. It makes the heart beat faster and harder night and day, asleep or awake, dead or alive.

On the first day of college, I weighed exactly ninety-nine pounds. My dedication to my calorie diary was finally working like a charm. My heartbeat accelerated, time slowed down, and nature began to relinquish her hold on me. I was euphoric. My clothes slipped over me like a breeze, and without the cumbersome folds of flesh, there was space for air, for wind. My feet were parting from the earth. The walls of the chrysalis disintegrated. The faerie slowly spread her raw young wings. She was free. She was me.

11. Size Zero

When I stepped off the bus on the first day of classes, the flurry of activity overwhelmed me. I wanted to die at the sight of all the confident young women and men who eagerly flooded in and out of the main campus building. They were so gorgeous. (And I was not.) They were bright. (And I could never be.) They seemed so eager. (And I just wanted to run away.) As students brushed past me, I took out my camera, put it to my face, and looked at the same scene. Through the magic of refraction, the campus winked at me and beckoned me forward. My camera was a second set of wings.

I was majoring in science—because that's what was expected of the "smart kids." The tedious formulas and calculations in chemistry class made sense only if they served me in the science of losing weight. By the middle of the first semester, I weighed ninety pounds. For that I gave myself a good grade.

By October, ochre and gold leaves hung off branches like toddlers clinging to their mothers' warm thighs. Autumn had only begun, but the winter-like air settled early into my bones. I secretly reserved a spot by a generous window in the depths of the library, a secluded and quiet place to hoard the sunlight and allow its warmth to sink into my tissue. During class breaks, I completed assignments and pondered over formulas, theorems, and equations until my head throbbed. In this private spot, my body withered from the world, and no one questioned why I dozed so much, why my belly growled so often, and why I wore so many layers of clothes. I flipped through pages of textbooks wearing gloves, and sat on a folded towel to prevent the wood from wearing against my bones and leaving bruises on my buttocks.

Halloween came just in time. I concealed myself in a cocoon of bulky wool sweaters and doubled-up underclothing. Hollow pockets of air filled my loose jeans. I shuddered in pain as the breeze bit into my bones while I waited for the bus with other students whose animated conversations no longer penetrated my consciousness. At lunch time, I'd catch girls from my chemistry class staring surreptitiously at me in the cafeteria with looks of mild revulsion and pity. They sat at the opposite end of the room, whispering about me, I was sure of it. I curled over my bowl of clear broth, first embarrassed, then angry. Finally, indifference overcame me as I gave myself over to the faerie, who remained deeply committed to her science project.

The science project results were progressing quickly. My body was mutating. One day, I caught my reflection in a window and didn't recognize the figure reflected back to me. I lifted my camera and took a picture of this creature with bulging eyes and sunken cheeks, insect-like, fey. Faerie existed. The burdensome identity I had carried for so many years had finally withered away, and the faerie had taken me over.

By early November, I weighed eighty-three pounds. My heartbeat slowed and my blood cooled. Tears no longer flowed. The faerie didn't worry about the future, didn't dwell over the past, didn't fear who she was becoming and what she was going to do. And she never thought about Mr Black.

My routine was carefully planned and strategic. I had to devise ways to bypass Mother and her food, for her maternal drive had been kicked into high gear. Zipping through the house to the front door never worked. As the faerie slipped out of the bedroom and fluttered toward the door, there was Mother blocking her in the hall. "No you don't," she'd say. Faerie threw a tantrum, hitting and flapping her wings in protest, but mother blew the weightless creature right back into the kitchen.

I woke up each morning at six, did sit-ups and squats, weighed myself, showered, drank black coffee, skipped breakfast, argued with Mother about skipping breakfast, took the lunch she had prepared, and avoided her pained eyes as she asked me to promise her to eat everything. These impossible lunches—sandwiches, containers of yogurt, bananas, cookies, and juice—ended up in the trash can at school. At the end of the day, the evening meal and Mother were waiting with greasy chicken curry, basmati rice, *aloo gobi*, two buttered *rotis*, and more pressure to eat every single morsel. I complained about the grease and made declarations about what I had eaten that day.

"Everything?" she insisted.

I'd show her the empty containers, dumping loose crumbs from the bottom of my lunch bag to convince her. But she could see that her child was starving to death, and she was absolutely powerless to stop it.

At seventy-eight pounds, I no longer had a period. Where my breasts once were, only an outline of my ribcage appeared. Any soft roundness about my thighs had vanished magically, and my brittle hair lay in dull clumps, which I strung into a thin braid.

My mother dragged me from doctor to doctor trying to make meaning of my insanity. The doctors prodded and poked, asked pointless questions, and confirmed I was suffering from "poor appetite." All I needed was to eat "more protein," "more iron," "more calories." Mother took their prescriptive advice and got busy in the kitchen cooking red meat (no more feeble chicken curry). Meat would be my medicine, she decided, but I declared myself a vegetarian.

"Anorexia nervosa." The foreign words rolled off Dr Fortin's tongue. The doctor looked at me from behind his enormous desk in his office at Saint Catherine's Hospital. With hands clasped in prayer, he asked in a deep voice, "Do you know what that is?"

"Yeah, I know. And so?"

He reached for a pen and pressed the tip against the desk as if to assert his point. "*That is* what you have."

"Is it serious?"

With a slow blink, he nodded. "Over my thirty years of practice, I have seen young ladies like you die from this, and not in a pretty way. Do you want to die?"

I froze and stared, shifted my body away, and inwardly rolled my eyes. Did he think I was stupid enough to admit that and get myself dragged into his asylum? I got up and left his office. Of course I had read about anorexia in *Seventeen*, in tabloids with scandalously bony starlets, had heard of a few who'd died from it and others who'd emerged from the rabbit hole in one piece, healthy and scarily plump. I had nothing to do with *that* diagnosis. I just didn't care. If death didn't scare me, then nothing could. Not caring was my middle finger to medical intervention and indeed to Mother Nature.

I sat in the lounge watching the doctor speak privately to Mother. "No beds yet," and "You will hear from me soon," he'd said, among other things. She nodded a great deal, shook his hands with both of hers, and bid him goodbye. She strode toward me. I stood up, but she didn't stop and continued past me, out the door. When I turned to look back, the doctor was gone. The office was empty. No Mother, just me and my impotent middle finger.

On our way home, she didn't look at me or say a word. Was she giving up on me? The streets glistened with steely blue wetness that caused cars to scream eerily as they drove by. When we reached the house, Mother stomped up to the door and walked in as though I wasn't there. She didn't switch on the lights but went straight through the dark hallway to her bedroom and shut the door.

I passed the night in an abyss of longing. I had rejected my mother in childhood and built a fortress inside me. Now, I think, she was protecting herself; any day I could be dead.

A week later, in mid-sentence while I spoke to a cashier in the supermarket, my heart stopped. I fell to the floor and all went black.

Part Three:
Metamorphosis

12. Phase Zero

All psychiatry patients are put into Phase One upon admission. They graduate phases until they reach Phase Four when they are discharged and released back into the world and into their roles and routines, the offices and households from which their damaged selves were plucked. In each phase, there is a set of rules that patients must abide by.

All patients, upon admission, are put into Phase One—except for me. My mental disorder was determined to be unusually unyielding. It was triggered not by brain chemicals or a genetic condition. My madness was simply the pure and irrational urge to undo nature. For me, a special Phase was created—Phase Zero. These Phase rules were tailored just for me here at PACU:

PHASE ZERO: Bed rest. Solitary confinement. Door closed except for meal times. No visitors, no phone calls. No reading or writing materials. No TV or radio. No bathroom privileges. Bedpan use in room only. Showers permitted ninety minutes after meals.

PHASE ONE: Solitary confinement. Door can remain open. No visitors. No reading or writing materials. Access to PACU lounge once daily for ten minutes. Two phone calls weekly, maximum ten minutes. No bathroom privileges.

Bedpan use in room only. Showers permitted ninety minutes after meals.

PHASE TWO: Visitors permitted once a week. No reading or
writing materials. Access to PACU lounge twice daily for
fifteen minutes. Four phone calls a week, maximum fifteen
minutes each. Limited bathroom access. Showers permit
ted ninety minutes after meals.

PHASE THREE: Bathroom and PACU lounge access. Showers permitted at anytime. Reading and writing materials
permitted. Unlimited phone calls and visitors allowed.

Daily caloric intake: 3,000 calories (3 daily meals + 2 cans
of Ensure)
3 pound weight gain on weight day: Graduate a phase
Less than 3 pound weight gain on weight day: Lose a phase

I had been in the PACU for four weeks. My weight gain hovered
between 1.2 and 2.2 pounds at every weight day, so I was still in
Phase Zero. I now weighed 71.21 pounds.

The only therapy offered to me was with Dr Messer during
rounds and with my nurse, who sat with me for a few minutes
each day so she could have something to report, then call it a
day. Fortunately, after a month, I was no longer obliged to attend
weekly group therapy sessions with other patients on the fourth
floor. In the last session I'd attended, a patient pointed at me,
called me "skinny bitch," accused me of taking up a valuable bed,
and said I was starving myself just for attention.

Being in solitary confinement suited me just fine. I used those forty-five minutes a week no longer wasted in group therapy to plot ways to get rid of as many calories I could. I had been secretly hoarding away food, stocking it up under the mattress and furniture and floor tiles. Thanks to my regular routine of secretly hiding food and emptying all light-coloured liquids into the bedpan, I had been doing away with thousands of calories. There was probably enough food in my room to feed the entire floor. Most mornings, during my late-morning shower, I could manage to sneak out only a few items—a few slices of toast, a muffin—which I concealed in my skimpy towel and buried in the deep and ample bathroom garbage bin. I calculated that I had been doing away with 1,500 calories daily, making my total intake exactly that: 1,500. This fifty-percent balance somehow reassured me that Dr Messer and I were even; we were head to head. It was a truce. For now at least.

"Good afternoon!" Nurse Personality didn't bother to knock. I wouldn't earn that privilege until I was off bed rest and had graduated from the currency of three added pounds. I sat upright, forced my eyes open. She was looking more pregnant each day. She opened the blinds and let the sun flash into my eyes.

"I want my camera," I blurted.

"Get to Phase Three, then you'll get the camera." She dropped the tray of food onto my tray table. "They didn't have green salad, so I got you carrot and raisin salad instead," she said.

What gall, replacing an innocent green salad with that greasy, sugar-laden dessert they called salad, then expecting me to swallow it without objection.

"I don't want the carrot and raisin salad." I crossed my arms over my chest. The feel of my ribs pleased me. I was proud of the work, time, and effort it took me to develop that bone and eliminate the breast.

"If you don't eat the salad, you'll have to make it up somewhere else. If you don't, it will go on your record. You didn't make three pounds last weight day, Lila, so you'd better think about this."

"There is a difference of eighty calories between green salad and carrot salad."

"There will be no negotiating," she told me.

"I'll have a Melba toast."

"There will be no negotiating."

"I'll have apple juice instead of the salad."

We argued more heatedly until she gave me an ultimatum. "I'm going to call Dr Messer."

I agreed to eat the salad.

Exhausted and angry, I nibbled away. Feeling sick, I shivered as my lips touched the oily, cloying sweetness of the grated carrots. I chewed, swallowed, and cringed as numerous horrid button-sized raisins scratched against the back of my throat. I hated them; I hated those useless pieces of desiccated grapes that I'd spent hours of my life plucking out of muffins and cereals.

Nurse Personality stood watching me as I ate. I had the uncanny feeling that she got a thrill from seeing me fattened up before her eyes, especially as her once-slim figure thickened from her pregnancy. I saw her tugging at her tightening belt, perhaps in a moment's recognition that her body was swelling up and there was absolutely nothing that she could do about it. I seemed to be more loathsome to her as that baby grew inside of her. The rest of the staff was just as hypocritical, always comparing dieting tips and secrets and exercise trends, always competing in some contest of self-control as they encouraged me to put on weight.

When I'd finished the carrot and raisin salad, she took my tray and walked out. What followed was a silent tidal storm within me. Within half an hour, as I lay on my back with a full belly, a nightmarish torrent of guilt ensued and lasted a gruelling eighteen hours. I spent the day in a corner of my room—one the nurses couldn't see unless they came in—unrelentingly running, skipping, and burning off that four-ounce salad.

Tomorrow was weight day. I was afraid to gain. I was afraid to lose. I was stuck in an irreconcilable middle. Between the fear of gaining weight and falling short, I faced the possibility of tougher restrictions or reliving the onslaught of guilt and anguish all over again. Which was worse? Dr Messer had warned me that if I didn't gain on the next weight day, I'd be force-fed another 1,000 calories daily with a feeding tube and sedated until I had put on fifty pounds. Fifty!

At night I lay awake. I was not permitted to have a clock or watch in my room, but considering the turbulent relationship I had with time, it was just as well. After lights out, I could recognize the regular pulse of reverberating sounds in the hospital corridors and neighbouring rooms—cascading water within the walls from running taps and flushing toilets, the murmuring of staff and sleepwalking patients. Like a ball tossed into the air, at the zenith of its ascent, there was complete blissful stillness for a moment before it began its inevitable descent. The window then seemed to grow when dawn filled it with light. The hum of distant buses and trains rose as the world geared up for rush hour. Doors opened and closed, and the hallways echoed with the shuffling of soft shoes and low murmurs as the tired night guard exited, replaced with a rested one. The clicking of heels became incrementally louder, sharper. A brief pause at the door, then, "Lila, it's weight day."

I made the three-pound gain. I was relieved. I was devastated. I had gained exactly 3.21 pounds, making my total weight 74.21 pounds. Nearly seventy-five. Less than I had weighed in grade five, more than I could support at eighteen. Despite the relief that came from not having to be tube fed, the shock of having gained so much weight, even on 1,500 calories a day, brought on my usual guilt and desperation. I was paralyzed physically and psychically drained.

Ninety minutes after breakfast, I was permitted to shower. I didn't want to disrobe and see my bloated nakedness, but I had to get rid of the hoarded food, which was already creating an odour in my room. I was worried that the cleaning staff might have wondered about it. I neatly crammed as much food as I could into two rolled-up towels, tucked tightly under one arm, made my way to the bathroom, and locked the door. I dumped the food into the garbage can and covered it up with a thick layer of scrunched-up paper towels. Then I ran the shower and dabbed some water onto my hair so that it would look as if I'd showered.

I graduated to Phase One. I had earned the privilege of leaving my bed without repercussion. I could roam my cell and scrutinize each floor tile and try to distract myself, if only temporarily, from my fanatical obsession with calories, food, and weight. I counted exactly 134 tiles in my room. The north-east corner tile was particularly yellow, and water damage had created an unusual mosaic of deformed faces on it. I stood dead centre on tile number fifty-six, and in six minutes, lunch would arrive. I was so lonely and scared I could die.

Finally, after three weeks of isolation in the hospital, I was about to speak to my mother for the first time. I was allowed a ten-minute phone call. I sat in the cold nursing station and felt my hot breath against the receiver as I began to dial. My own phone number became entangled in my mind with the digits pin-balling around in my mental library of calories. I hung up and crossed my arms, then tried again.

"How have you been, Lila? Dr Messer tells me you have gained a little weight—"

"Yeah," I interrupted her. "I also went up a phase."

"Ooooh!" Mother exhaled like she'd been holding her breath for months. "You see, you can do this, Lila. I know you can."

My body melted in my chair.

"Did you go to the bathroom? Are you pooping alright?"

"Yes, Mother. I haven't pooped like this my whole life."

"What did you eat?"

"A lot. I ate carrot and raisin salad. It was awful."

"You see? If you were home you would be eating proper food."

Then I heard Dad's voice.

"Hello, hello. How are you? Did you gain, then?"

"Yes, Dad."

"Excellent!" Then a beat of silence. "Okay, then. So when can we come to visit?"

"When I get to Phase Two."

"Good." More silence. "Have you been taking pictures?"

"No, I'm I not allowed to have my camera."

"Why not?"

I twisted the phone cord around my finger. "That's Phase Three."

Suddenly, a burly patient threw himself over the nursing station counter, jerking a peace sign with his yellow fingers. He was due for his cigarette. Nurses collected around him, then an orderly and a nurse's aide arrived and escorted him away.

"Lila? Are you there?"

I missed what my father had said. Nurse Personality tapped her watch and spread her hand, signalling five. Mother took the phone back from Dad and crammed in as much as she could as we counted down to zero minutes.

Four: "Do you need any clothes from home? Are you warm enough?"

Three: "Are you getting enough sleep?"

Two: "I'm sure that the worst part is over, Lila. You will get better now. We'll have you home in no time."

One: "Yes, yes," I replied dutifully, soaking up the sensation of her soothing voice.

Zero: "Come home soon." My ten minutes were up.

13. Hard Lessons

My weight gain stalled around the seventy-five-pound mark. The subject of my weight became a great concern to staff who knew nothing of my secret hoarding schemes. Surely I should be packing on the pounds on a 3,000-calorie-a-day diet. I was either up to no good, or my body had defied science.

No one confronted me, but I received more frequent inspections and got the feeling that they were plotting a set of tougher rules and regulations, perhaps an increase in calories and a decrease in freedom. To prevent this, I wanted my weight to nudge up a tenth of a pound at least.

During the changing of the guard, when the staff convened for reports, there was a delicious window of opportunity when I could safely do a rigorous workout and burn up to 200 calories. My senses were hyper-vigilant while I continued my secretive regimen, which had become stressfully elaborate. I'd been waking up at two a.m. and jogging in place. I would then do 300 jumping jacks followed by 500 sit-ups. This had been my routine for weeks now, along with hiding and hoarding food. I was burning roughly the calories that I imagined a healthy, vivacious girl my age would on a Canada Food Guide diet.

But unexpectedly, my weight dropped to 69.6 pounds. The staff was alarmed. I had tempted fate and taken things too far. Dr Messer retaliated by putting me on a diet of more solid food.

My darling clear juices, destined for the bedpan, were replaced with fruits and yogurt. I had to eat more carbs and more protein. But he didn't suspect that I had anything to do with this weight loss. How on earth could a girl stripped of everything and confined to a room and bed lose weight?

Special physicians came and went who poked, prodded, and palpated (but did not poke under my mattress). They took a CT scan, robbed my blood and urine, and came back with a report: No cancerous cells, no tumours, no disease (other than madness). No plague to report back to my poor dear mother.

Then there was silence. I didn't hear a word from the staff for days. No more specialists came to visit the expert anorexic. In the meantime, the effect of the solid food diet began producing the most stinky gas and unbearable throbbing cramps in my intestines. I hadn't been to the bathroom for four days, and with each day that passed, the discomfort grew. I was given Colace, a stool softener, and prune juice (containing ninety-two unwanted calories), and then Metamucil, which bloated me further. By the fifth day, my stomach was rock-hard and grotesquely inflated. My body was unaccustomed to real food after my steadfast regime of diluted variations and substitutes empty of calories and nutrients, all of which glided through my indifferent intestines. On the seventh day, I was in agony. I sat on my bedpan in the shameful dark, and for over an hour I pushed and forced and struggled with a hardened little nugget in my anus that jabbed against my skin until I bled. I cried and then gave up.

For the remainder of the afternoon, I sobbed silently, curled up in bed. I had, after all, only myself to blame. As I lay there,

Dr Messer's words echoed through the mental clamour of self-pity: "You can't stand yourself." I couldn't absorb the words any more than my intestines could digest solid food, yet those words continued to ring during moments of stillness when I was most helpless and silent. I didn't want to gain weight. How could I let go of the ecstasy, the rush of accomplishment that came from doing away with flesh and fat and the burden of bulk?

"Hello?" Nurse Personality knocked against the opened door with a manicured hand. She stood in my doorway, forming a long, sleek shadow into my room. "It's only eight o'clock. What are you doing in bed already?"

Out of curmudgeonly annoyance, I turned away without answering, but she marched over to the bed, felt my pulse, and checked my vital signs. Sitting down next to me, she said quietly, "Didn't manage a bowel movement, did you?"

After a moment, I turned and looked up at her. For no reason that I could explain, I cupped both hands over my face and began to weep. Then, with an unexpected tenderness, she pulled me against her and brought my floppy head to her lap.

"Oh, honey, hard poop is a hard lesson, isn't it? But nothing to cry about!"

I laughed, thrown off by her playful sympathy. I could feel her belly against the back of my head, pressing against me.

"You see what you've done to yourself? I'll bring a clean bed-pan, and you can try again tomorrow. We'll make it alright." She began to stroke my hair. "When I was your age, I wanted to be perfect. I thought I could be. But if I had known that life was going to set me straight, no matter what, I wouldn't have made myself so miserable trying to be in control all the time." She bent to look at my face. "See what I'm saying?"

I looked up. Nurse Personality's voice registered, but the words slipped through me like air. Her golden hair had lost its lustre, her complexion seemed bloated and tired, and her movements had become lethargic and heavy. She slowly stroked my hair, wrapping it behind my ear, and I didn't want her to stop. I didn't want her to stop being kind to me. I fell under the hypnosis of her touch, and that night I rested and had a dreamless sleep.

The following day, Patricia (I had stopped calling her Nurse Personality in the night) had no choice but to get into her latex gloves and wrangle out the hardened faeces from my sore rectum. To my surprise, this repulsive exercise was one that she approached with dignified professionalism. She came in, shut the door, and got down to business. At this point, I was ready to tolerate any pain, discomfort, or humiliation to find even the mildest relief. I got necessarily naked and on all fours on my bed. Through the window I saw what appeared to be a dead body encased in white sheets being placed into the mortuary van in the inner courtyard. I dropped my head and thought, *This is not how I imagined my life at eighteen.*

"Are you okay?" she asked.

I looked back at her and nodded. Then I prepared for the worst.

"Okay, now. Take a deep breath, then exhale and push as hard as you can." I followed her instructions, she gave me a few reassuring words, and within minutes the job was done.

"There. You'll start feeling better now." Sloth-like, I cleaned up and slipped back into my clothes. I wanted more than anything to thank her. I watched while she picked up and collected everything and waited for the right moment to say a few heartfelt words. But with hardly a glance at me, she made a quick exit. I sat frozen on my bed for a moment, puzzled and disappointed. Replaying the event in my mind, I wondered if I'd done or said anything to upset or trouble her. But then I just assumed that she was preoccupied and had a busy day ahead. It made me sad to think that I was just another patient to tend to, a chore to accomplish, and was no more special than anyone else.

I got up and lumbered slowly to the door, my bottom sore, and went cautiously into the lounge. It was empty. Inching my way to the nursing station, I heard a strange noise from inside. I peeked through the main door. From behind a filing cabinet, I glanced down the hall and into the nurse's bathroom. The door stood slightly ajar. I saw Patricia's back shaking in spasms as she coughed. Morning sickness, I told myself. That explained why she'd left abruptly. She stood upright, turned swiftly, and caught me looking at her. Tears streamed down her cheeks. I jumped back and returned quickly to my room.

By midday, when lunch arrived, I was served by another nurse. "Patricia had other business to tend to," I was told. I asked if she was sick, but she shrugged. I shifted my focus and spent the rest of the day as I usually did: registering calories, burning the ones I digested, and disposing of the rest—and making dead certain no one noticed.

"Lila, Lila." The bed boat rocked and the sky opened onto another strange realm where a flock of numerical digits flew over the horizon and a sea nurse called my name. "Lila. It's snack time."

The biscuity odour pulled me from my watery dream. There was Nurse Patricia, who I was delighted to see. I sat up, realizing that I had been napping for an hour; my diet of solid food and cocktail of antidepressants had made me tired. I calculated the caloric difference that an hour made between being awake and burning calories and drifting in the make-believe sea of excess calories, and I decided to do jumping jacks for an extra seven minutes once staff met for report. I had it all figured out before I was fully awake.

Patricia lingered for a bit. "How are you?" she asked. "Have you been to the bathroom?" Her manner was cool again. I told her that the Colace was working.

"Good," she replied without meeting my eyes, and began walking to the door.

"Is everything okay?" I asked.

"Why, yes," she said with exaggerated surprise. She could see from my sidelong glance that I didn't believe her. She came back and sat down next to me.

"The other day when I had to, you know, relieve you of your pain … " She paused and lowered her voice. "I got quite upset."

She told me that she became physically sick from seeing my body, my emaciated buttocks, throbbing blue veins, the dark bruises on my lower spine (from innumerable sit-ups), my bleeding anus. All the parts of me that I had become blind to had made her sick.

For the rest of the day, I thought about what she'd told me, and her words troubled me in ways that I struggled to understand. This was the effect that my appearance had on a professional who I thought would be desensitized to the sometimes gross physical signs of patients' illness. But I also felt a strange satisfaction that my body could provoke such a reaction. I had succeeded in creating a body that was so skinny that it was hideous enough to drive people away.

Why did I feel that way? Why was I half living? I was teetering over a dangerous chasm, between life and death, between those two universes, and I didn't want to belong to either. But at some point, I would fall one way or the other.

14. A Measure of Secrets and Loathing

The diet of solid meals created more than just constipation; it created an unsolvable riddle. Unlike liquid nutrition, the solids couldn't be expelled from the bowels or thrown away as easily. I had accumulated a stock of soggy sandwiches and mouldy muffins whose odour led staff to believe it might be coming from exhaust fumes blowing from the main kitchen. I used the new diet to justify my more frequent bathroom trips so that I could dispose of the stockpiled rotting food.

After breakfast, I waited for the morning staff meeting to ask the new nurse's aide, Harry, an easy one to trick, if I could shower. He shrugged and carried on with his crossword puzzle. Thank you, Harry, very much. With hands trembling, I stuffed as much food as I could into two large towels and cradled them like overfed babies in my arms. I crossed the sitting area past Harry and saw, through the office window, the staff collected for their meeting. Just then, Nurse Patricia turned her head, and her eyes landed on me. I lost my hold of one of the towels, and a few crumbled soda crackers fell out. I shut the door behind me, not daring to see whether my secret had been discovered.

I wrapped the food in paper towels and tucked it deep into the trash can, then scattered crumpled paper towels on top. As I performed this ritual, my memory curled back to a routine that my hands and gestures were way too familiar with. What I was doing with the unwanted food reminded me of the way Mother had taught me to dispose of used sanitary napkins. The procedure was carried out with the same measure of secrecy and loathing. I would tightly roll up the napkin and wrap it in a long strip of toilet paper (the length of paper was directly proportional to the amount of shame the hidden object provoked). Once the coast was clear, I would slip out of the bathroom, silently and secretly make my way to the main garbage bin in the kitchen, and tuck it under all the "clean" and "proper" garbage, making sure it was totally hidden. I would leave feeling absolved, until my body produced another unsightly discharge that needed sanitizing and disposing of.

"Are you done? I need to pee real bad." Nancy, the forty-something patient, was scratching at the bathroom door.

"Can't you wait? I'm about to shower—"

"No! I can't!"

I quickly topped up the trash with more crumpled paper towels.

"Now!"

I opened the door and Nancy barged in, dropped her drawers, then plopped herself on the toilet and began to pee. I stepped back in shock. Harry came to my rescue, nudging me out, then shutting the door to let Nancy have some privacy. Just then, the nurses emerged from their station, holding their trays like cocktail waitresses about to serve their customers. I quickly scattered the cracker crumbs on the floor with my foot.

After lunch, the pasta and tomato sauce bulked up in my

belly (this was a meal I could not hide in paper towels), so I writhed and counted calories in my familiar state of boredom and guilt. Boredom was not merely a feeling of discomfort brought on by the lack of stimulation. It was the sister of depression. My thoughts looped continually over numbers, calories, weight, and unstoppable guilt. I worried about being forced into consuming even more calories or being medicated to the hilt like Nancy. I wrangled with the crazy, chattering monkey in my brain, telling me how fat I was, how worthless I was, what a failure I was to myself and to my family, and even to my malady.

I could obediently submit—eat, gain the weight—compliantly follow the program, and get it all over with. I could surrender to the doctors, to womanhood, to my future. To life. And for what? To be "normal"? I couldn't relinquish my joy over my emaciated limbs, the exalted emptiness of my belly, and the rush of power that came from defying the dreadful gravity of adulthood. The faerie held on.

After 200 leg lifts and 500 sit-ups, my abdomen was hard and my composure restored. What had I been going on about? Submitting, surrendering? Never.

I heard voices from the other room and footsteps scuttling back and forth. I slipped off my bed and shuffled to the door. Nurse Patricia emerged from the bathroom wearing yellow rubber gloves. In her right fist was a garbage bag. Then she disappeared behind a wall.

I walked backward and crawled onto my bed, replaying in my mind what I had just witnessed in those brief seconds.

My attention zeroed in on the plastic garbage bag. Was the evidence of my deceit bouncing inside? Or was it merely an innocent sack of laundry heading for the cellar?

It was past four p.m., and the cleaning staff hadn't yet scoured through my room, emptied the garbage, changed my sheets. Voices became louder, and then I heard Dr Messer's leathery drawl break through the monopoly of female voices. Outside my window, the van was fed another corpse before heading to the mortuary. Why hadn't my body given up when I'd called upon it to do so? My eyes scanned the room, hungrily searching for a sharp object, a weapon—a way out. But all I had was a shrunken bar of hospital soap, a toothbrush, a bottle of shampoo, a jug of water, and a plastic cup. Even my prison wouldn't allow me to punish myself. I was so angry that I'd let myself get caught.

I covered my face with my hands. Between my fingers, I could see shadows and reflections of people intruding on my private retreat. Then the commotion stilled, and there was silence. I slowly lowered my hands, looked up, and saw the floor staff assembled at my doorway; they were all staring at me.

Dr Messer took three solemn steps in my direction. He cleared his throat before speaking and in a stern voice said, "You have disappointed me again. You know what I'm talking about. You broke your end of the bargain. What do you expect will happen now, Lila?"

"I don't know," I whimpered.

"There are two things that can happen. We can discharge you now and let you die, because you will soon, anyway, or we can get tougher on you. And you'll live. Those are your two options."

"I promise I won't do that again. I'll be good." I started to sob.

"I don't give a damn about what you *say* you will or won't do. I don't trust you. I don't trust what comes out of that mouth of yours." He stood erect, and seemed to grow a foot taller. "You're eighteen, legally an adult. You can sign the papers and leave whenever you want. There are plenty of patients who would gladly take your place and welcome our help."

I shook my head and continued to cry.

"What? You like it here? What do you want?"

"I'm sorry. I'll be good. I'll be good."

He turned back and signalled for Nurse Patricia to step forward. She hesitated, then came to the side of my bed and dropped the bag to the floor. A putrid stench filled the air; in sync, the nurses cringed, covering their faces.

Dr Messer pointed to the bag and said, "*That* is time." I looked at him quizzically.

"Five, six weeks, in my estimate. You would've been half way out the door of this place, had you eaten what you were supposed to."

Did he not understand that this was no simple equation for me? How could I explain the fear and repulsion, the self-hatred that a serving of carrot and raisin salad produced in me? A slice of cheese was as catastrophic as cancer. Did he not understand that food was a grenade, detonating an onslaught of anxiety, guilt, and self-loathing inside me? He must know this; he was the professional.

"I feel very bad when I eat," I said.

"What do you feel bad about?"

"The calories. The weight. Losing control."

"I am sorry to tell you this, Lila, but you lost control a long time ago."

I buried my head in my knees. All I wanted now was his approval. *He will forget my blunder and give me another chance*, I prayed. *And love me. Love me like a daughter.*

"Do you want to get better, Lila?" he said softly.

"Yes. Of course I do."

Dr Messer looked at the floor and nodded. "I was naïve. I should have known better." After a moment, he said, "Lila, I cannot discharge you. You know that. Your weight is dangerously low. From now on, you are going to be tube fed." He turned and headed for the door.

I leapt off my bed and ran up to him, begging him to give me another chance.

"No more free rides." His eyes darted to the foul-smelling bag, and he left the room.

The day after the discovery of my hoarded food, a group of interns entered with the specialist and his rubber hose. "How're you doin' today, miss?" the specialist said as he rolled the tray table over and set up his supplies. He was a smiley, moon-faced man, plump and middle-aged.

"So, what's a gal like you doin' in a place like this?"

I gave him a silent and grim glare.

"Looks like somebody slept on the wrong side of the hospital bed!"

I wanted to punch his dough face but forced a smile instead.

He picked up a stretchy tube, less than a quarter-inch in diameter and extending to … it looked like eternity. I imagined the journey it was about to take inside me. The tip was fastened with a capsule-sized piece of something silver.

"C'mon, feel it. It's soft," he said. He held the tube out to me as though he were getting me acquainted with his pet snake. I squeezed it between my fingers; it felt wet and slippery and softer than I had expected. Placing the tube on the tray table next to a plastic cup of water, the specialist handed me the cup and instructed me to drink.

"Will it hurt?" I asked, feeling a dryness build in my throat.

"Nah. Nothing a young lady can't handle. Just like getting your ears pierced."

I squeezed my eyes shut and gulped the water as he poked the rubber up my nostril while lullabying, "Nice and easy, nice and easy." I sneezed and coughed, and the tube tumbled out. He told me to relax my facial muscles and swallow more slowly. I swallowed the water and felt the tube slithering down the back of my throat. The sensation was unlike anything I had ever felt, and its weight seemed to pull my sinuses out of my head. Once the ordeal was over, I opened my moist eyes and noticed the end of the tube dangling like a massive Rajasthani nose ornament from my nostril.

When everyone had left the room, I sat up on my bed. In the window's reflection was a girl whose life was about to go in a different direction; her body had been taken over and no longer belonged to her. The numbness I felt that day quickly turned into terror once the lights went out. In my sleep, I wrangled and fought off hands and limbs, boys and men groping me in my dreams. The rage I felt was so terrific that I forced myself awake, shaking off memories that haunted me in my sleep. How could I escape my own memories? The feeding tube would be a trigger; it was a leash, a constant reminder of my submission to my master, the very thing that I despised. It produced a continual twenty-four-hour drip of calories, the equivalent of six 250-calorie cans of Ensure, at the rate of 62.5 calories an hour, and all the while I was on bed rest. I was not even allowed to walk around in my own room except to use the bedpan. And I'd been told that having the drip didn't mean that I could stop eating. I was still required to eat three meals and three snacks every day.

I braced myself for what was about to hit me in a few hours, when the food had entered my stomach and begun to shape into flesh, bone, and fat. How could I keep the faerie creature alive, the precious miserable faerie, who now would be stripped of her wings and sent to earth?

15. Angel of Death

The morning bustle of staff in the hallway shook me out of my sleep. I was no longer in PACU and had been transferred to the main floor of psychiatry where I'd made my mad escape in February.

The Phase rules were different on the main floor than in PACU, and inevitably, special rules applied to me. I was on Phase One, and "would remain there until the feeding tube was removed," Dr Messer insisted. If the unwanted calories weren't punishment enough, the feeding tube kept me locked in miserable Phase One. Dr Messer wasn't taking chances. He did say, however, that he would permit me privileges along the way, depending on my behaviour and weight gain.

For seventy-two hours, the plastic pouch had been hanging upside down beside me like a bat in hell's cave, trickling nutritional supplements into my esophagus. In the last seventeen hours, I had consumed more calories than during my greatest binges when I was sixteen and suicidal. My feeding bag had shrunk and collapsed, but the thick, creamy fluid still snaked inside the tube, which looked like a vein under the transparent skin of a cadaver. It starved itself as it fed me.

"How is Lila this morning?"

I didn't bother to turn in the direction of this new voice. I heard the squealing of the plastic bag being squeezed out of its hook and replaced with a buoyant refill. My wings fluttered then beat like a trapped insect against the window pane, thrashing against the glass.

"It's Monday. That means porridge 'n' raisin toast."

The nurse cast her broad shadow over me, obscuring the window as she balanced the breakfast tray under my chin. I could tell from her brusque manner that, although she was a seasoned professional, she was likely unaccustomed to dealing with a delinquent creature whose gravest foe was food.

She touched my arm in a way that startled me; it was firm and earnest, and in an alert and tender voice she said, "I know it ain't easy, hon. Just take it one meal at a time."

I looked up and scanned her face, which was round and full and cocoa-brown. I guessed from her accent that she was West Indian. I watched her robust hips as she swaggered to the door with a heavy gait. She must resent me for being so fierce and rigid. A sad casualty, she must think me, of the great white North American lean dream machine.

"I'm Jean. I'll be your nurse now. You eat or I'll be givin' you a good beatin'!" With a wink and a chuckle, she was gone.

I shoved the tray away and noticed a huge, horrific bulge in my stomach. And if I refused to eat? I would be fed a richer, more fatally caloric supplement through the tube, night and day, asleep or awake. I would grow bigger and heavier, regain all the weight I had worked so hard to lose. The faerie had been captured in the hunter's net, and the enemy would pin her into the collector's casing.

I was sluggish all day and sleepless all night. At two in the morning, I stared unblinking at the shadows on the wall and lay motionless on my bed, bracing for flesh to form and skin to stretch and inflate my body like a circus balloon. I sank deeper into my mattress. I could detect this from the way each curve and crevice along my spine and thighs settled more completely into the fabric of my bedding. The gaps and funnels shaped by bone against skin, through which wind and air had circulated freely, were closing and incrementally filling up and anchoring me further into the earth. And without more sedation, I was subject to subtle and terrific palpitations as each new layer of flesh formed and eliminated the elegant, gaunt angularity I'd worked so hard to achieve. I kept touching my body, feeling the changes, pinching new tissue around my waist and forearms. My thighs had already become soft, my hips enlarged—after only a few days. I slapped my hips and grabbed my tender new breasts so hard it hurt, for they'd appeared without my permission, invading my body like malignant tumours. I punched my gut and a storm of grief gushed out, but my clumsy, bloated body resisted my pleas. It was now conspiring against me. I was shackled to this feeding apparatus, my wings disintegrating, collapsing against my growing flesh. I had to stop it. I had to burn it. That night, I burned it off by jumping and jogging in place. I exercised throughout the night. The faerie had once again made her escape.

The rumble and squeal of rubber tires broke through the brief bubble of sleep I'd managed to get after exercising. Under my door, a rapid flicker of shadows glided across the floor like a train steaming past a forgotten station. I crawled out of bed and scrambled toward the door, only to be jerked back by my feeding tube. I grabbed the pole, wheeled it to the door, and peered out.

At the far end of the corridor, orderlies rolled an empty stretcher into the elevator. I realized that the room next to mine was occupied again. I couldn't recall a patient being admitted at such an hour before.

The rules said I was not permitted out of my room. My curiosity did not respect those rules, I said to myself. I slipped out with the feeding pole and made my way to the next room, where there were four beds walled off by grey curtains. I noticed an enchanting draft billowing out from the nearest curtain, luring me in. I moved toward it and parted the gap in the drapery. The high bed at first seemed empty, but under the flattened bedding lay a wafer-thin body. I moved closer and saw a tangle of brittle unruly hair of an old man or woman, and the side of a gaunt face. Just as I moved away to leave, the head slowly turned toward me. Hazel eyes bulged out of a skull-like head. I realized at once that this was no old woman but a girl about my age. Reddish-blue gashes railroaded along her sunken cheeks, and from under the bedcovers, a bony arm bandaged up to the elbow dangled out.

I parted my lips to utter a "Hi" or "Sorry," but nothing came out. The girl lay there with hardly enough strength to speak a word, let alone see. She shut her eyes and rolled her head away from me, tucking her naked arm under her like a shameful secret, as though I'd stolen something from her with my gaze.

I retreated to my room and thought about the girl, wondering what had led her to this madhouse. Was she a faerie cousin like me? My initial concern turned quickly from empathy to envy, however, because my frail neighbour had outdone me in emaciation, had made my meek dietary restrictions look like child's play. I had to do more to weigh less.

For days, after seeing my new rival, I was fired up. I paced back and forth from one wall to the opposite, dragging my feeding pole, unwilling to yield to the bed, unwilling to bow to the will of calories, except when the enemy was heard coming. Then one afternoon, a strange scratching noise caught my attention. A corner of yellow paper poked underneath the door. I walked over and with my big toe dragged it toward me and picked it up. I read the badly spelled writing: "I know your jumping. If you don't stop, I'll tell. Sorry but just saying coz I don't want you to get hert. Alyssa."

I put down the paper and threw open the door. Who the hell was Alyssa? Then it hit me that this might be the name of the new girl next door.

I slammed the door shut. "It's y-o-u-apostrophe-r-e, you dumb girl, and h-u-r-t, you witch, you skinny, conniving b-i-t-c-h." Who the hell did she think she was? How could she possibly know about my night-time exercises? All I could hear when I pressed my ear against the wall were the low hum of voices, the rumbling of furniture, and the clanging of pipes, which could very well have been from the hallway or from my intestines digesting breakfast. Not only did she discover my secret when no one else had, but she had the nerve to poke her nose into my business and threaten to call me out.

Her sly intrusiveness seemed to suggest what I most feared— to be revealed for who I really was: a fraud. My "illness" was no illness at all, but as the patient in group therapy had pointed out, a grab for attention. To my fragile inner self this girl was saying: "I know you better than anyone. I know your next move, your tricks and manipulations, and you cannot deceive me. I will reveal your true face." In a matter of minutes, she had exposed me like a raw nerve. I resolved to be more vigilant and quiet when I exercised at night.

For the rest of the day, I bounced and burned off dinner with lunges and leg lifts and did a springy cardio routine memorised from a workout video. I made sure to do the jumping at the opposite end of the room from my rival. After my ninety-minute cardio routine, I opened the door for air, and there she was, standing before me, this spooky child, like the angel of death. "Hi." The edges of her pencil-thin lips curved upward strangely; her wide, unblinking eyes remained as lifeless as a mannequin's. "I'm Alyssa." She leaned forward slightly. What did she expect—to be invited in for tea?

I saw that she was as skinny as I was, but her calves were thick and muscular. Instantly I was relieved. I was still the winner in my mad contest of emaciated Olympics. Yet her frame was identical to mine; she and I were the same height, and she was endowed with a frailty like mine. In her hazel eyes, I thought I could detect secrets. She was a creature of great power and melancholy, I knew it.

"So what's with the note?" I said.

Her eyes grew even wider. "Well, I was worried you'd faint or something."

I tried not to cringe. I would not bow to her fake concern.

"Look, maybe you should just worry about yourself and mind your own business." I shut the door just as I noticed her lips parting to produce words. But I shook her off like a bad dream. Then, a few moments later, I felt bad. What if she was being sincere? What did I know about her life, the suffering she may have endured in her seventeen or eighteen years? Maybe she needed a friend. For the rest of the day I was preoccupied by her. Was she friend or foe?

However, I continued with my secret exercise regime. Defiantly I jumped and ran in place at night and burned, over the course of three hours, approximately 450 calories. After a rest, I took it up again a few hours before breakfast. On our weekly weight day, I'd get to see how my efforts would stand up against the calories forced on me. But how much longer could I keep it up? My ankles were starting to feel sore from hitting the floor so hard in my ratty slippers. I was tired, I was achy, and wanted badly to sleep at night. But I continued, simply because I had no choice.

On weight day, nurse Jean nudged me awake at seven and led me to the scale. I couldn't bear facing it, so I stepped on it backward, looked upward, and prayed.

"If you keep goin' like this, sugar, you'll be out in no time," said Nurse Jean.

According to the scale, "sugar" had put on 3.23 pounds. I was still on Phase One, but Dr Messer said I was now permitted out of my room to stroll in the great corridor of the sanatorium in the faithful company of my feeding pole. But this hardly made up for the fury that ran through my bones. I would take solitary seclusion and weight loss over all the privileges in the world rather than be burdened with three greasy new pounds.

My heart sank like an anchor in a sea of disappointment.

That evening I got so weak and tired I could hardly move. I felt my body sink slowly and completely, and I fell into a deep, paralyzing trance. My eyes were open and I could see, but I had left my body and drifted away from time and reality. Then I swelled up with a crushing loneliness. This sparked the image of Alyssa's hazel eyes, a void into which I sank, eternal and boundless; it left no opening, no light. The following morning I awoke on the floor, feeling as though I had died in the night. I believed this incident was a sign, a warning to me that something terrible was about to happen.

That evening, I passed Alyssa's room again and heard a low sobbing and the rustle of papers. I walked in and nudged through the curtains. A waft of pungent antiseptic assaulted my senses. Alyssa sat with her back toward me. On her bed was a mountain of newspapers, and her arms were working at something I could not make out.

"Alyssa," I said quietly, but she didn't hear. "Alyssa."

She stopped and twisted around to look at me. Her eyes were bloodshot and her face both gaunt and flush from what seemed like a marathon of crying. I saw that she had been ripping up the newspapers.

"It hurts," she whimpered.

"What the heck are you doing?" I walked in closer.

She shook her head and cried some more.

"I can't. It hurts too much. But they say I gotta get stuff out."

I shook my head. "I don't understand."

"I have twenty-two left," she said, weakly continuing to tear the papers.

I noticed that her fingers were black from ink and bloated like mini-sausage rolls.

"It's supposed to help me with my urges." She raised one bandaged arm and looked at me, rolling her eyes. Her arm dropped again like falling timber.

"I can think of a million other things they could make you do, other than this stupid thing!" I said, outraged on her behalf. There was a photo on her bedside table showing a young girl with rosy cheeks and thick, shiny hair, wearing shorts and hiking boots and standing on a cliff.

"That you?" I asked.

"Yeah," she said, stopping in mid-tear and looking at the photo. "I was thirteen. I scaled Mount Washington with my dad." She turned to me. "I was so different back then. I didn't have these ... urges." But one day, she said, she just snapped.

"So here I am. And I have to tear fifty newspapers a day." She kept ripping.

"And what if you don't?"

"What do you think? I'll have fifty more."

I dragged my feeding pole over to the bed and sat down next to her. I began to rip one paper at a time, which, I figured, might burn a few calories.

"Thanks," she said, looking directly into my eyes.

"So why are you here?"

Her eyes darted away. "They said I was a danger to myself."

"So am I."

"Yeah, I know," she said without missing a beat.

The question I was dying to ask her—how she knew I was jumping in my room—now seemed stupid. She told me that when she turned fourteen, her personality changed like a light switch had been thrown. She became severely depressed and attempted suicide twice before grade nine. Her diagnosis? It changed as frequently as the dress size of a pre-teen girl. During each hospitalization, the specialists came up with different diagnoses, and neither she nor her family knew what in the world was the matter with her.

"How long have you been in this place?" she asked.

"Too long."

We sat there companionably for the rest of the evening, like factory workers shredding papers. I hadn't realized how lonely I was for a friend until I had her company. It gave me time off from my own maddening thoughts. It was strange to hear my own voice as I spoke to her—I rarely spoke to anyone except the nurse. That evening, I felt a meagre sense of sanity and humanity, but beyond that I felt like I knew Alyssa, like I had always known her.

At bedtime, I helped her stuff the torn papers into a garbage bag. We took it to the nursing station where it was inspected by her nurse. I asked Alyssa how they knew that she had ripped exactly fifty papers.

"I don't cheat," she said.

I watched her walk back to her room. She stopped at the door. "You wanna hang out tomorrow after breakfast?" she asked.

"Sure."

She raised her bandaged arm with a wave and a smile, and disappeared into her room. Over the following weeks, Alyssa and I became almost inseparable. We shared secrets. She pointed to places within me that had meaning, and I did the same for her. The qualities of our light and dark made us who we were. She was my sad, true soul sister.

16. Butterflying Woman

I was still in Phase One, bound to my feeding pole and obliged to wear hospital garb, but now that my weight had begun to climb, I was permitted the scariest new privilege, which didn't feel like one at all, and hit me hard.

"You're going to have to learn to get comfortable eating in the company of others," Dr Messer said. I now had "cafeteria privileges."

I was used to eating by myself. It allowed me greater control over how I could strategically starve myself and not be affected by the appalled and shaming reactions of others. But in a cafeteria with heavily medicated patients, I would have to find new and inventive opportunities to get rid of food. One of the better known side effects of some medications was an increase in appetite. I thought it wouldn't be that difficult to lure a patient or two into relieving me of a piece of apple pie or a date square. This new privilege would work to my advantage—so I thought.

On day one of enjoying my privileges in the Four East cafeteria, I joined the regular lunch line-up of fidgety patients with my tray in hand and felt their nerves reverberate throughout my body. The hall was steamy hot, and a humid sticky air of cooking clung to my flesh. I honestly believed that I was absorbing calories through my skin from the dense smell of food. It made me crazy. The sweaty server dropped a bowl of creamy mushroom soup onto my tray. Then she added a plate of turkey slices soaked in thick, mocha gravy with a mound of mashed potatoes and a dribble of mixed vegetables. I struggled to hold the tray up with one hand, as the other had to manoeuvre my feeding pole. The server then slapped two thick slices of white bread on top of the turkey. I froze, horrified, looking at my food. It felt like I had been assaulted, not served. An onslaught of objections went through my mind: I had never asked for gravy. And did it need to be so thick? I didn't ask for mashed potatoes, either. Why the white bread? Why not brown? Why any bread at all? I looked up, and the woman behind the counter stared at me.

"Is everything all right, dear?"

I stared with rage but held my tongue. I expected the ordeal to be over, but then a bowl of carrot and raisin salad landed on my tray.

"NO!" I screamed. The room went dead silent.

A nurse rushed over and took the tray from my hand before it fell or got smashed into someone or something. "What's wrong?" she asked.

My body went hard, arms stiff along my sides, fists clenched. "No carrot and raisin salad," I growled.

She looked at my tray, then at another nurse who had joined us. Picking up the bowl, she said, "Salad. Gone," and removed it from my sight.

With my tray in her hands, she led me to my designated spot, where I could be observed closely by staff. I dragged my feeding pole along with me and sat, still in shock. The nurse bent down and looked into my eyes to examine my pupils.

"You okay now?"

I didn't respond. I noticed her scribble something onto a clipboard. A few moments later, when she left the report on the table to tend to another patient, I read: "12:13 p.m. Patient became extremely agitated when carrot and raisin salad was served to her. She calmed when it was taken away. Perhaps a trigger of a traumatic childhood incident?" I snorted in derision.

Suddenly, Alyssa sat down next to me with her tray, oblivious to what had just happened. She smiled and nudged my ribs with her elbow. "You're here! We can eat together now." Alyssa dug into her meal. "No one ever wanted to hang out with me at the school cafeteria."

My body flooded with warmth; I was immediately comforted. Soon I began to experience the true benefits of public eating, thanks not to therapy, but to my new friend.

Yet as my weight climbed, so did my anxiety levels. Dr Messer's therapeutic visits had become surprisingly rare since my steady weight gain; besides, he was busy treating a new crop of patients who had been admitted. I was invited to begin therapy with Dr Bélanger, who had been assigned to take on my case for an interim period. The last thing I wanted was to be trapped inside the office of another grumpy expert and fed his psychoanalytical mumbo-jumbo. I politely declined the doctor's invitation. But that did not stop the doctor from inviting himself over.

I heard a knock on my door, then a woman's voice. "Can I come in?"

The doctor was not at all what I had expected. She strode in and stood next to my bed and gave me a warm smile.

"Hi, Lila. I'm Dr Bélanger. You can call me Eileen."

I stared at her, speechless.

"How are you feeling today?"

I sat up. "Not great," I grumbled, still taking her in. She looked to be in her early thirties and had wheat-gold hair that tumbled onto her shoulders.

"Why didn't you want to come see me?" she asked.

"Because." I lowered my eyes and mumbled, "I don't trust shrinks."

She nodded, chuckling.

"What's so funny?"

"That's hardly surprising. Maybe I can do something to change your opinion of them. That's partly why I became one."

She sat down beside me and said, "It's a long boring story, but when I was about your age," her eyes darted around the room, "I was exactly where you are now. And when I got better, I decided to become a 'shrink,' to help young people. Like you."

I was shocked by her candour. I wanted to know more about her, but she turned the focus of the conversation back to me.

"I heard you have a creative streak," she said.

"I do?"

She handed me the canvas bag she'd brought with her. "I asked Dr Messer to let you have art supplies to draw and paint with."

I poked my head in the bag and took out a sketchpad with pearly smooth pages, a batch of pencils, and a watercolour paint set.

"I asked for your camera," she added. "But that will have to wait till Phase Three."

"You asked for my camera?"

She nodded. "Lila, I want you to know that my door is open. You can come and talk to me anytime you want. I'm only here on Tuesdays, though. You miss me then, you'll have to wait a week."

And she turned and left.

It took no time for me to "eat up" my new privilege of painting and drawing. I sat on the bed and sketched a massive portrait of my new camera as I remembered it, now locked away in my closet. I filled it in with paint, dabbed on a generous dose of glitter, ripped it out of the sketchpad, and stuck it on the wall at the foot of my bed. It was magic. I felt high.

I thought about Dr Bélanger for the rest of the day. I discovered from Nurse Jean that she was well-respected and apparently had even received some research grants. But what fascinated me most was that she was a grown woman who had emerged from the rabbit hole in one piece. Maybe she'd once been a faerie who'd metamorphosed and transformed into a butterflying woman, with a bigger, stronger set of wings. I pondered that and let it sink into the back of my fairy tale brain.

Alyssa, meanwhile, had graduated to Phase Two. On the main floor, that meant she could wear her own clothes, as all patients could at that phase, except for me. That was when I was in for a shock.

One afternoon, someone stepped into my room. At first glance I thought, "Who is this boy? He must be lost," but it was none other than my freckle-faced faerie sister. She wore straight-legged Levis and a plain sweatshirt and her hair was tucked into a beat-up baseball cap. She emanated no sex appeal, no style. And yet her expressions and gestures had the refinement of a dancer, a lightness and frailty that was incongruent with her rustic, androgynous appearance. Like me, she had an almost neutralized sexuality.

She sat on my bed during the mid-morning lull, her body slumped into a c-curve, examining her cuticles, picking away at loose skin, then biting it off as though she were squeezing slivers of thoughts out of her mind.

"Breakfast was shit," she said. Her leg shook and rattled the bed.

"Shit from calorie hell," I replied, pacing the room with my feeding pole.

"So, how come you're still on Phase One?"

"They like to keep me in their fat farm, that's why."

"Phase Two is nothing much, so who cares."

She was right. The freedom that a phase allowed didn't make up for the torment that weight gain brought on. We were growing comfortable there, citizens of the insane asylum; we would be foreigners in the world outside.

I picked up my sketchpad, sat down, and started to draw a picture of her. "What are you going to do once you get out?"

"What do you mean?"

I didn't answer but continued to draw. I was afraid of what she'd say. It had already been more than a month since she'd been admitted, and I realized how little I knew about her. What was

her family like? Did she miss them? Our conversations had orbited around our mental health, the medications, nurses, other
patients, and, of course, the lousy fattening food. My connection
to her was deep, but it had never crossed my mind to ask about
her life outside this place. I knew that family was a sensitive topic.

I braced myself, and out it came: "How come your folks never
come to visit?"

A flush of blood rose to her temples. "And how about yours?
Haven't seen them either," she shot back.

"I'm just asking."

She sighed. "They're sick of coming here, I guess." After five
hospitalizations, Alyssa's parents had apparently grown weary of
the routine.

Would my family tire of me? Would I exhaust their supply
of sturdy love?

"C'mon. Let's get outta here." She hopped off the bed and
headed for the door.

For the rest of the morning, we paced the hall, watched nurses and interns shuttling back and forth, patients lumbering along
at half speed. We poked fun at everyone, blew spit balls, and
lifted the burden of all questions off our minds for as long as we
possibly could.

17. Gaining Pains

"Honey, don't let it get you down," Nurse Jean said gently when she found me one morning on the floor, sobbing hysterically against the radiator. "Cheer up!" she said. "It's like breaking in new shoes."

I began to resent her upbeat tone; it seemed to dismiss the pain and horror I felt about the changes taking place in my body. What was getting me down was that my weight was going up. Bulging new flesh appeared literally overnight, wobbling on my midriff and rear. I had to pinch my skin to confirm that indeed it was my own. I had spent the night twisting into my mattress as I felt my flesh enlarge and bloat like an unwelcome stranger, my detestable twin, was emerging inside me. I vowed that when I got out of this place, I would follow the most extreme diet so that I could lose weight as quickly as possible; it would be like pulling the plug on an inflatable doll.

One hundred pounds would be the magic number, the one-way ticket, the eject button to the alien world outside. On the feeding tube and high-calorie diet, my weight started to increase more quickly than ever. Ninety-one, two, three, four, five, six, closer and closer, when suddenly I stopped gaining at ninety-nine pounds. My weight remained there for two weeks. On weight day, I was filled with dread, especially after sluggish Sunday when even more calories were slipped into my meals from larger and greasier portion sizes and were digested by my slowing metabolism. Surely I would tip the scale over the one-hundred mark.

On that silvery Monday morning, an oblique sunray beamed down the hall like a UFO headlight and onto the medical scale near the nursing station. Nurse Jean stood next to it, projecting a long lean shadow in her path. With a sharp flick of her wrist, she slid the weight with a sharp clank that made my heart stop. She turned to me and nodded. I held my breath and stepped onto the scale. One foot pressed onto cold metal, then the other. Shoeless. Breathless. Then darkness. I shut my eyes and saw uneven flickerings, golden speckles dancing behind my eyelids. I heard the sleek dragging of the metal slide back and forth. Then it stopped.

"Okay," she huffed.

I stepped off the scale and opened my eyes.

Nurse Jean scratched something into her chart then walked away, shaking her head. "Where them calories goin,' only Lord Jesus know."

The muscles in my face dissolved with joy. "Yes!" Fist in the air, I returned to my room walking lightly on my toes. I was still just 99.2 pounds. I had been complying with the program, eating exactly what I was told to. Dr Messer didn't lecture me or perform his therapy wizardry on me. Instead, I was wheeled off to get tests. But all results failed to indicate why I wasn't packing on the pounds. Dr Messer finally came to the conclusion that the cause was entirely psychological, and the culprit was my incredible inertia. He claimed that it was my mental and not physical state that put me at risk. That was the only thing we agreed upon.

But when he would sit and talk to me, I couldn't seem to reply; all that came out were feeble wafts that left me light-headed and exhausted as though all the air had been suctioned out of my lungs from the force of a few syllables. I had neither the strength nor desire for words. I had, in the depths of my being, silently made a decision to come to a halt at enigmatic number ninety-nine. Another week passed and still no change. The nurses took me on brisk walks on the main floor to stimulate me out of my stalemate. But another week passed, and I still weighed ninety-nine pounds.

Dr Messer strode into my room one morning during rounds. "If you don't change your attitude, Lila, I'm going to have to send you to the Dunhill." He let that sink in. The Dunhill Psychiatric Hospital was the mother of all mental asylums. "They practice the types of extreme … therapies there that I, in good conscience, could never bring myself to impose on my patients. Is that what you want?"

To that, I hardly batted an eyelash and looked at him with a mental yawn. Now that I was eighteen, and therefore legally an adult, and more or less within the so-called "normal" range of body weight, I could no longer be deemed a risk to my health. Dr Messer could, without consequence, discharge me from his care with the stroke of a pen. But I think his pride prevented him from doing so. Letting me go meant letting me win, and Dr Messer was a miserable loser—like me.

It was perfectly clear to me why my weight was locked at ninety-nine. One hundred was a triple-digit emblem that stood for completion, termination, a submission to nature and to whole-ness. It didn't match the fragmented, splintered state I was in. One hundred was dull and inert, while ninety-nine was dynamic and defiant. The number meant that I would never yield, never settle. The faerie was in control.

More daunting than weight gain was discharge. My curious condition was the result of rejecting a life that I had never laid claim to. I didn't feel that I deserved to be alive in the ways that other people were alive, outside the hospital. I cared not a whit for the privilege that I had been born into, with an able body, a mid-dle-class household, a family who provided for me and loved me.

In the fourth week of my clinging to ninety-nine, Mother, Dad, and Mina came to visit me. Mother and Dad spoke about how much they missed me and wanted me home, healthy and happy. Mother tried to cheer me up, flipping through a Sears catalogue and pointing to clothes in "healthy sizes" that she'd buy for me. But her tone and gestures were fatigued from months of hope, now throttled by my refusal to gain.

"Lila, when are you coming home?" Mother put the catalogue down, sighing.

"She's not. She's getting too comfortable here," Mina grumbled.

"How can she be comfortable?" Mother glared at Mina.

I just sat there, numb and overwhelmed. I couldn't say the words she wanted to hear: "Don't worry, Mother. I'm better now. I'm going to come home."

All I could feel was the torment of the new flabby flesh on my inner thighs, which rubbed against each other revoltingly. *If only*

I had a butcher's cleaver, I thought, *I'd slice the blubber from those thighs and toss it into the trash.* How could I explain the fierce power of these thoughts and desires? I believed then that Mina—and maybe Mother and Dad, too—wished I'd already killed myself so they could have buried me and gotten on with their lives. And who could blame them?

"I'm almost there," I told her. "Just a pound to a hundred ... "

"And then? What will happen when you come home?" Mother said wearily.

I looked up and caught Mina's eye. In the contours of her arched brow and firm lip (and short of flashing me the finger), I read the simple truth: she had grown up and I had not. What stood between us was time, and within it I was absent. I had missed her basketball games, her prom, and her birthday. Her big sister had not been there during the many times in the last year when she needed to lean on the experience and comfort of an older sibling. Not only that, I had stolen the spotlight away from her. "Fuck you, sister," is what I heard in the contemptuous silence of her look.

Mother sat staring out the window. Dad stood, hands deep in his pockets, his foot scratching away at some stain on the floor.

This was it. I had worn out their sturdy love.

"What's going on?" Dr Bélanger asked. Her office felt more like a living room than a clinical office. Plants cascaded from pots, and on the walls were canvases of calm, dreamy seaside scenes— blue skies and cottony clouds that I wanted to soar into and take flight. An Oriental area rug partly covered the scuffed hospital linoleum, and a collection of delicate crystal figurines of animals decorated her bookshelf.

"Lila?"

I looked at her kind, compassionate face, covered my own with both hands, and sobbed. I cried for what seemed like an eternity while she just sat there quietly. I was shocked at how I had just fallen apart. After a moment, I blew my nose into a tissue.

"How did that feel?"

I looked up at her smiling face and chuckled. "Well, better than Xanax."

She sat patiently as I told her about the family visit and how miserably it had gone. "I'm scared, I guess," I said.

"Of what?"

"Of the future. Of life."

"What scares you?"

"Everything, pretty much."

"Do you think you've given life a chance?"

"Yeah. Eighteen years of it," I said.

"Do you want to die?"

"I'm too *fat* to die."

"That shouldn't prevent you," she said unflinchingly.

I shook my head, about to write her off as just another Dr Messer, when she said, "If I had given up on life, I wouldn't be sitting here with you. It *does* get better."

I don't know why, but I believed her. For the next nine hours, at any rate, I believed her.

18. Art's Masterstroke

Dr Bélanger suggested to Dr Messer that Alyssa and I be allowed to try art therapy. So, after two o'clock tea, Alyssa and I walked down the long east-wing corridor, past the salty waft of soup from the cafeteria, until we reached a scene that could have almost emerged from memories of kindergarten. Circular tables and wooden chairs were painted in Lego colours. Bookshelves held dripping paint cans and lumpy mounds of clay. And the patients' collages, sculptures, and drawings were scattered about the room and on the walls—they were expressions of wounded psyches and broken lives, revealing a raw, sad beauty.

Alyssa and I spent an hour and a half in the art therapy room most days with other patients, moulding clay, beading bracelets, sketching flowers, painting portraits, and distracting our minds from the craving to cut, the compulsion to starve. On the first day, Alyssa threw her paint brush against the table and stormed out after ten minutes, grumbling and tired. I knew her urges had possessed her when the soft hairs of the brush pressed hard into the paper and produced a grotesque green blotch. I caught her scanning the metal objects other patients were using, assessing, I assumed, their bluntness and sharpness and the depth of imprint they might leave on the underside of an arm.

I could see that Alyssa didn't care much for art therapy; for her it was an obligation, as exhausting as ripping newspapers. I was able to see the silver lining in the dreary tasks of preparing paints, producing a cohesive image on canvas, or extracting a carving from soapstone because what I produced, I believed, had some artistic merit. Dr Bélanger had already planted the idea in my mind that I was an artist, and her words had power over me, more than I would admit.

By the second week, it seemed that Alyssa had begun to find some benefit from kneading her knuckles into folds of clay and cupping it to shape vases and bowls and lumpy heads. But as she told me, her art never measured up to the images she had in her mind. Her fruitless attempts to create something from nothing only served to expose her life as empty and hollow, without shape, beauty, or promise. A life of failure is how she saw it.

It was in art therapy that I began to wonder what would become of us. Once the suitcase was packed, discharge papers signed, and doors held open for us to walk through, what lay ahead? Our bodies would be recovered, the weight gained, the sutures healed. And our psyches? Would they have been mended? How would we hold up against the storm of reality, the demands of family and friends, careers and life challenges? How would we navigate all of the constricted passages through which girls must squeeze to become women?

Although there was nothing physically wrong with me and my weight stayed at ninety-nine pounds, I began to have head-aches, lapses of memory, and numbness. I went to Dr Bélanger's office, but sat there unable to speak or even cry. I had checked out, pinched myself off from all feeling. She didn't pressure me to say anything or answer her questions, but it was obvious that I was more agitated the longer we sat there in silence. My leg shook, my fists clenched.

"Lila, no one is forcing you to be here. You can go if you want."

I wanted her to force me to stay, to impose some harsh rule on me like Dr Messer would.

"One of the pleasures of being a grownup is that you're free to choose," she said. "Choice is power."

I sat there, paralyzed, unable to make up my mind. I complained all the time of being controlled and manipulated by others and by life circumstances, and yet when I was offered a choice, I couldn't make one. Finally, I got up and left. As I walked back to my room, I wondered if I'd done the right thing. I was on a precipice, not moving forward, not going back.

"They're letting me go," Alyssa told me in her room one day.

"You're joking!" I said as a golf-ball-sized lump rose in my throat. Alyssa, who had jumped from Phase Two to Four had, according to Dr Messer, complied with the program and not expressed an urge to harm herself. Therefore she was ready for discharge. What "urge," I thought, could she have when the most dangerous object accessible to her was a toothbrush?

I swallowed the lump in my throat. "So, when?" I asked.

Casually and half yawning, she replied, "Oh, um, day after to-morrow." She tugged at her bedcovers, smoothing out the wrinkles. I stood waiting for her to say more, but she went on fussing with mindless tasks while I became more annoyed by how cool she was. I threw myself on her newly made bed.

"Hey, what's your problem?" she said.

"*You're* cured? You?" I laughed. "You know as well as I do, you're not ready."

"You're jealous!"

"You don't even wanna get out!"

"'Course I do, stupid."

She shoved me off her bed and smoothed the bedcovers again. With her sleeves hiked up, her scars were exposed. Since the bandages had come off, her arms had been hidden under long-sleeved shirts that stretched over her wrists. I knew never to ask to see her scars, never to mention them to her. When she saw me staring, she pulled down her sleeves, strode straight into the bathroom, and slammed the door.

I walked over and tapped on the door. "Alyssa? Alyssa, I didn't mean it," I said, stepping back and waiting for her to answer me or come out. Moments later, as I turned to leave, dragging my pole with me, the door opened. She walked out and brushed past me.

"You don't get it." Alyssa threw herself in the chair and curled into a ball. "I'm just a fucking revolving door."

I stood there puzzled, not knowing what to do or say.

"Just leave me alone," she said. So I did.

At lunch time, she ate at the far end of the cafeteria from where I sat, and when she left, she glanced my way but wouldn't look directly at me. Alyssa didn't show up to art therapy. Forty-eight hours away from discharge, she was no longer obliged to. I stared at her newest shapeless clay figurine. It was wrapped in wet cloth, ready to be moulded into a form, any form. I took it into my hands and resuscitated it, made it my own. As I did, her absence forged deeper crevices of loneliness inside me. I missed her voice, the sound of her laughter, the warmth of her understanding—how wrong it felt that she wasn't there. I was incomplete.

For the rest of the afternoon, she either kept to her room or huddled on the phone having voluble conversations, making plans, marking off her agenda with dates, parties. And when she saw me coming, her body twisted away and into the receiver. As I walked past, I held up her clay sculpture. Her eyes stuck to it for two seconds, as though I were carrying her baby, then rose up to meet mine. She looked away, brushed her hand over her face, and curled into the phone again. After dinner, I couldn't imagine how I'd endure another day without her company. I didn't want the night to end, for in little over a day, she'd be gone. I dimmed the lights and lay on my bed and wondered if this was the end of our friendship. Neither of us had the courage to talk about it, it seemed. Would we be like travellers who met in some foreign land and, once our journeys ended, parted ways forever? Was this how Alyssa saw our friendship—as transient and disposable? Maybe I was just someone to keep her entertained while she laboured through the dull days in hospital, and she didn't feel about me as I did about her. Had I merely conjured up a fantasy of who we were to one another out of some pathetic, abject loneliness?

An hour before lights out, I opened my eyes to see Alyssa standing in my doorway. She shuffled toward me as I sat up, her eyes swollen like mine. She sniffled and wiped her nose with her soiled sleeve. We looked at each other and began to laugh.

Alyssa picked up her sculpture and said, "Damn, that thing is ugly."

"Sure is ... What should we call it?"

She stood before it, scratching her chin. "How 'bout Alila? A mashup of our names."

"Cool." After a moment of silence, I asked, "So what did you mean earlier, about a revolving door?"

She scratched nervously at her wounds. Bulging salmon-pink lines turned white when she scraped her nails into them, and small scabs still clung to her flesh. I wanted to pull her hand away, worried she might bleed.

"I've been in and out of this place so many times. But this time it feels different." She turned and looked at me. "I'm not coming back."

"Well, that's good news," I said brightly. She looked down, and then I understood her perfectly. "Don't say that." I reached out for her hand, but she jerked it away and continued to pick and scratch, dig and peel at her scars.

"And you? How about you?" Her eyebrows twitched when she looked at me. "How do you feel about getting out?"

"I'd rather die than gain weight."

We stared at one another but didn't say a word. She got up and went to her room. Lights out.

"Lila, wake up." Breath smelling of mint toothpaste woke me from the underbelly of a dream. "I have a plan!" Alyssa said as I sat up.

It was early, barely seven, and the nurses were still preparing for the day's shift. Alyssa announced that she'd had an incredible vision during the night. It was as though pieces of a puzzle had fallen into place.

"Our lives," she explained, "have been lived out to their fullest extent. That's why neither of us can see a future for ourselves, right? Lila, our time here, and I don't just mean the hospital, is over. I'm sure that we met here because we're both being called forth into … the great infinite realm." She met my astounded gaze. "It's time, Lila. It's time to end it."

"You mean," I ventured, "we should …"

She frowned at me as though I'd completely missed the crucial meaning of her point. "It's not just that! It's much *more* than that." She explained that time had no more use for the bodies we were born in. We had come to time's end. I sat back and let her words sink in.

Of course, had I not been the faerie creature whose earthly passage had led her into this insane asylum, this would've sounded like complete insanity. But it not only made sense, it seemed as though my destiny had finally been revealed. Within twenty-four hours Alyssa was to be discharged. Her parents would be arriving to take her home in the morning.

"I'm not going to be here to see them tomorrow," she said. Her last conversation with them would happen later that day over the phone and then she and I would carry out our plan. I nearly fell to the floor. She wanted to do this today.

This had to be a calculated operation. The method: poison. The poison: shellac. The place: art therapy room. The time: 14:30 hrs. The result: death. The destination: paradise.

We would steal into the art therapy supply room, each take a container of shellac, and drink the poison.

"It'll be done in minutes." She spoke like a plumber faced with the job of unblocking the kitchen sink. My throat dried out, as though her words had already set in motion the effects of the poison.

"Tic Tac?" she offered.

I took the candy.

"What does shellac taste like?" I asked, sucking the mint.

She shrugged. "Dunno. Probably a lot like Pledge."

It was remarkable. While planning her death, her essential nature had risen to the surface and the fog of bewilderment and gloom had been blown away with a bolt of practicality. I'd never seen her so alive and serene. For once, she stopped picking at her scars.

After breakfast we sat like Siamese twins on the lounge sofa that stank of coffee and tobacco, watching *Sesame Street*. Electric shivers ran up and down my limbs when my eye caught the great hand of the clock pulling time closer to the moment when we'd take our final breath. We flipped cards, playing Crazy Eights as Big Bird led a train of singing schoolchildren through the neighbourhood. My thoughts swirled back and forth in time, leaping television and game, space and memory, calculating numbers and calories and siphoning each moment that arose. Today's number was nine. Nine kittens, nine dolls, nine lives. She deals nine of spades. No more weight to gain from now on; I would become a ninety-nine-pound corpse. Nine cartoon children lined up in a row counting down to one. Backward. The hand moved closer to noon. *All my cards have been discarded. I win.*

I was giddy with fear and couldn't make myself speak to Mother or Dad on the phone. I thought of them only superficially, as something from the past that didn't belong to me. I felt little or nothing for them. Why was that? Had the inevitability of my death not sunk in? Had my mind, my heart, gone dormant in order to save me from sabotaging my suicide?

"You don't have to, y'know." Alyssa's grey eyes glimmered, eyebrows raised.

"If I didn't have to, I wouldn't. But I want to." I reminded her that months before she was admitted to Four East, I had fled the hospital on the coldest day of February and attempted to end my life.

"Maybe it wasn't time for you yet. Like it wasn't for me." She sat back and put her arm around me and drummed her frail nail-bitten fingers on my shoulder.

During lunch hour in the cafeteria, the swirl of faces and voices and the thick Saltine odour were brush strokes that were beautiful and repellent. My tray was already in my hand. How did it get there? I couldn't remember the sequence of real-time events that led me to the long line-up at the food counter and being served by Sam the Somalian who always looked upon me with pity. ("So sad, so skinny. Will never find a husband.") I would pass on dessert—lemon cream pie with its tart, pungent perfume. I looked at the Thursday lunch of red tomato soup, leafy side salad toppled with garlicky croutons, and a tangled pile of cold spaghetti. *My last meal*, I thought, and it wouldn't be my mother's cooking.

I sat next to Alyssa, who was staring at the lunch as though she'd never seen food before. I suddenly realized that not once since the morning had I worried about weight or calories. I told Alyssa, saying, "Isn't that amazing?"

"See?" she said knowingly. She was right; this must be divine destiny.

We were minutes away from art therapy. Alyssa looked at me and reached out, extending her hand. Her wrist was exposed, her wounds raw. I looked up at her.

"Wait. I have to pee," I said.

I headed to the bathroom. Once on the toilet, I couldn't go. The urge felt pressing and real, but it was merely a ghost sensation, brought on by a weak bladder, cold drafts, jumpy nerves—preparation for a suicide.

What was going on? What was I about to do? My mind went blank, then my gaze landed on the garbage bin. I stared at it for awhile, recalling how I'd stuffed food deep into it, day after day. I replayed this action in my mind and chuckled—it seemed crazy now. I sensed something missing, a crucial sound. Had my heart stopped beating already? I looked up. My feeding bag had gone dry, and its steady drip had stopped. I was about to go to the nursing station to get a refill, then caught myself. Wasn't I supposed to be doing something important just about now? I had to make a choice. And suddenly I realized that I didn't want to do this. I wasn't ready to die.

I rushed out, but Alyssa was gone. A wave of panic followed by a sense of angry betrayal came over me. I ran to the nursing station and screamed, "Alyssa! She's going to kill herself!"

A cavalry of nurses raced down the corridor with me on their tail. When we got to the art therapy room, Nurse Jean pulled me back by the shoulders and barked, "What the heck is going on?"

I twisted out of her grip and looked into the room. Nurses and aides were moving about frantically, shouting orders at each other. Nurse Jean pulled me away forcefully, backed me against the wall, and shook me.

"How did you know?" Shook me again, harder. "How did you know?!"

"She, she, she ... " I sucked up air as I sobbed. A stretcher whizzed by, and I caught a glimpse of Alyssa. Her face was blue and bloated. I remembered the first night I'd seen her; she'd been wheeled in the same way. I told Nurse Jean about our plan. She held me as I wailed, "I was going to do it too!"

"The poison got to her. She couldn't be saved." Jean's voice was steady, but she was trembling as she delivered the news to me. When she saw that I'd noticed, she pursed her lips, stood taller, and busied herself replacing my feeding bag and bustling about, being my nurse. My eyes followed her around the room, watching her every move, hungry for comfort. I wondered if she blamed me, held me responsible for Alyssa's suicide. As the thought crossed my mind, she gave me a look of disappointment, as though she'd read my mind.

"My shift is over. I'm off till Monday." She left swiftly and shut the door. A hush fell in the room. I held my breath, feeling Alyssa's absence. I wanted to weep but told myself that I had no right to. Alyssa was dead. I was not. And nothing would bring her back. Guilt sucked me into its quicksand.

Within twenty-four hours, Alyssa's room was cleared and another patient had moved in. I stood and stared at the bed where Alyssa had sat digging into her skin, picking at her wounds. Now it was occupied by an old woman with wild auburn hair. She shuffled around with a shampoo bottle in her hand, unsure where to put it, as though it meant the world to her. How strange, I thought. How fleeting. Who *does* care if you live or die? You take your life, and life goes on.

I heard voices down the corridor. A nurse was greeting a couple who had just come in. I saw that the woman was tall and delicate. The sturdy man next to her had his arm around her firmly, as if she might fall over at any moment. Alyssa's parents? The woman's hands clasped her face; I recognized that gesture. I could vaguely hear the nurse as she told them what had happened to their child.

"Who?" asked the woman. The nurse paused and looked down the hallway at me. My instinct was to duck back into my room and hide, but I held my ground. The woman's gaze fell on me. She broke away from her husband's grip and approached me. To my surprise, she put one arm around my shoulder and cupped her other hand against my cheek.

"Lila? It's okay. It's not your fault. It's not your fault, understand?" Then she pulled me into her arms and held me. I don't know how long she held me, but it wasn't long enough to convince me that I had not, in the act of not intervening, been responsible for Alyssa's death as though I had killed her myself.

Perhaps I felt that way because … Alyssa's mother didn't utter those words. Nor did she hold me, let alone look at me.

The following day, I didn't leave my room after getting weighed. I'd lost three pounds, but it meant nothing to me. I curled my feet up into my chair and pulled a blanket up to my chin. Nurses came and went, trying to console me, distract me from my anguish, and refocus my attention on my weight gain. But I couldn't stop crying. In my mind, I repeated over and over, *I could've saved her. I should've saved her*.

Eventually I remembered that moment in the bathroom when I made a clear decision to live, to part ways from my faerie sister. It meant something. It *had* to mean something. Alila, our clay sculpture, sat on my bedside table, hideous and incomplete. I had spent hours in the art therapy room trying to beat it into a shape, resuscitate something that was getting hard and solid quickly. It was a race against time. But I had failed to save my friend's life, let alone her art. I wanted to smash the object to pieces, but it was the only souvenir that I had of her.

I could start a new piece, I thought, an object unencumbered with our history. It felt crucial for me to do so. I remained in that chair for hours until light turned to dark, when I looked up to see a figure in the doorway. It took a moment to recognize her. The translucent vision of Alyssa floated in and passed through me like a spring breeze. By morning I awoke on my bed with my chest open and filled up with air. My breath was full again. I knew then that my sister's soul had crossed over peacefully.

"Why didn't you do it?" Dr Bélanger stood by my bed, her hands in her trouser pockets. I found it hard to look her in the eyes.

"The question is, why did I let her do it," I replied.

"That's not the question I asked."

I sighed and turned to the window.

"You blame yourself," she said.

"A hundred percent."

"You're giving yourself way too much credit."

Her words were beginning to ring true. I wasn't convinced that I was responsible anymore. I could no longer hide behind another story of guilt, a reason to sink into self-pity.

"I didn't do it because of what you said!" I blurted out. "Choice is power, you told me."

"Oh, Lila. Come here."

I looked up at her; her arms were held open for me. I got up and collapsed into them, crying. After I'd calmed down, she said, "If you'd put as much focus and determination on creating the life you wanted as you did in losing weight, girl, you'd be flying."

19. Blank Beautiful Slate

Day 362. Three days short of an earthly year is how long I had been on planet Four East. On this notable triple-digit day, I weighed 100 incredible pounds but was told that I would not be discharged until I could maintain this weight for a period of two weeks. On this auspicious day, which I mentally called "Fat Friday," Dr Messer put me on Phase Three and cut the umbilical cord to my medical mother. The feeding tube was slid out of my esophagus and the feeding bag put away.

I was also allowed a weekend pass, the first since admission. A weekend pass was given to patients so they could experience the pleasures and terrors of the world outside the ward for an experimental two days. I was in a state of fragile bliss—and panic. I would be going home and spending the days with family and nights in my cosy bedroom on rue Bordeaux.

Strangely, I could barely remember what my bedroom looked like. A girl's bedroom was supposed to be her palace, her shrine, where she could be allowed to blossom. But I was not blossoming, and my identity didn't have a clear form. I could hardly remember the details, the hues and objects that I had carefully arranged, the books on my shelves. Aside from my photographs, what was meaningful to me? I couldn't recall.

I watched Nurse Jean prepare for my weekend visit. I hadn't seen her this chipper and chatty since the Four East Christmas party, when (after a few spiked punches) she had performed a bouncy "Jingle Bells" in the rec room before the zombie-like patients with their frothy mouths and unblinking stares.

"You got to keep up the eatin'—and no cheatin,' alright?" she said as she packed. If I started to lose weight again, she reminded me, the feeding tube would go back in. Her West Indian accent became stronger when she got tough on me and when she was being extra kind to me. I responded to this because I was the child of a Punjabi mother who did exactly the same thing. Perhaps all ethnic mothers shared the distinctive linguistic code of communication that guaranteed desired results: Punjabi for scolding, nagging, and complaining or for sweet and endearing cooing, English for all else.

"What's this?" Nurse Jean bent down to reach into my locker. She pulled out a small square box, the blue wrapping paper still covering it. My heart skipped a beat as I took it from her.

"Am I allowed to have it now?"

She shrugged as she folded and tucked clothes into my suitcase. "Don't see why not."

I opened the box. My Leica. I felt at once both perfectly alive and absolutely afraid. "I'm taking this."

My heart raced as I stood at the double door on the main floor waiting for Dad's car to pull up, feeling the crisp morning wind on my skin for the first time. I wore my real-world uniform, clothes I hadn't had on for months. My jeans were snug now and rode up my thick thighs, pinching my waist, reminding me of my disease, and the brassiere poked into new folds of flesh that had formed under my ribcage. How would I endure living with this weight? What would I eat? *How* would I eat?

It was impossible. I wanted to spin around and return to my cell, to the great institutional indoors, where it was predictable and stale and where nature could not, with its shapeless, unyielding power, obliterate me. But I didn't give in. I stood upright, my camera hanging around my neck, a talisman that protected me from my maddening fear of the world. I convinced myself that I could, with the power of this apparatus, project my life as I willed it to be. I would point and take aim at the world.

I madly snapped a hundred images with my hungry neglected camera. Imaginary snapshots, as the camera had no film in it. I tried to ignore the tremendous fear that was building each second that I waited for my father to arrive. The earth rose slowly, devouring my ankles as my weight pushed against gravity. Wingless, I waited in the body of a grownup woman. And then Dad arrived, perfectly punctual in his new metallic-blue Ford. As he stepped out of the car, I darted toward him and threw my bulky woman's body into his unsuspecting arms.

When Dad and I arrived home, Mother was out grocery shopping with Mina. We stood silently in the doorway to the living room, side by side. This was the right address, but the house seemed to belong to someone else.

Velvety red wallpaper covered the walls, and our couches were now embellished with pillows and throws with Indian designs, squiggly paisley patterns in saffron and mustard. A saccharine sandalwood-incense odour hung in the air; I could hardly breathe. Dad explained that this redecoration was a part of something bigger that had taken place with Mother. When I was admitted to the hospital, she'd fallen into a deep depression. After months of listless melancholy, she found solace at the Gurdwara and in the holy teachings of the Sikh gurus, and she began to embrace her faith and culture. Mother's surge of spiritual devotion inspired her passion to redecorate the house. I thought the room looked like a mobster's den in a '70s Bollywood movie and silently prayed to the sixth guru that her inspiration hadn't led her into my bedroom.

"Don't worry," Dad said, seeming to read my mind. "Your room is safe." He grinned.

My room was as it always had been—a work in progress. The walls were winter white, with ash-grey wall-to-wall carpeting and the light, inconsequential Ikea furniture found in so many suburban North American homes. The room was an incongruent appendage to the rest of the house, as perhaps I had been to this family.

I walked in and sat on my bed. The space seemed indifferent to me, and in some way, that was comforting. I stood up, raised the camera to my face, and panned around the room, hoping to discover something original, startling, and special that my naked eye could not detect.

"Lila? Are you here?" Mother's soft heels quickened as she came down the hall. Her head peered in, her wide eyes searched around, then she noticed me in the corner and came toward me.

She took me in her arms, and then I felt at home. The home I had returned to was her.

That afternoon, I watched my mother's gleaming face as she pulled from her closet a wardrobe of clothes she'd bought for me. She was unearthing months of hope and longing for me to return home and be where daughters ought to be and not in lonely hospital rooms raised by psychiatrists and their expert rules. Suddenly I was longing for the expert and his rules, for the impersonal foster care of my nurses—and I'd been home for only a few hours. I had grown accustomed to the sonic universe of the hospital, which like a fairy tale castle, had shielded me from the movement and bustle of the ordinary world, the drudgery of day-to-day survival. But I no longer belonged there. Everything that was solid in me was turning soft and fluid. My skin's pores were opening and the new reality seemed to be gushing in and flooding my body with its meaning. Who was I? Where was I? Mother could see that I was getting anxious, so she closed the closet doors and said three magical words: "We have time."

And the time had come. The aroma of Indian cooking had been building like a pressure cooker all day. Mother had spent the day busying herself in the kitchen—I could hear the orchestra of clanging pots, closing cupboards, and ringing timers. Meanwhile, I had sat stiffly next to Mina in the den watching TV, with hardly a word to say. Her new frock flared like petals on the couch and I noticed that her fingertips glistened with a fresh coat of frosty pink nail polish. Did she dress up especially for me?

"Are we expecting anyone for dinner?" I asked.

"No." She looked at me. "Just you."

I obsessed over the sensation of my blouse seams pressing into my upper arms as I considered the upcoming meal and its unwanted calories. The thought unnerved me, so I shook it off.

I turned to my sister. "Hey, can I see your graduation pictures?" I asked suddenly.

Mina turned to me, surprised. "Sure." She sprang up, pulled an album from the shelf, and sat on the couch next to me. Pointing at photo after photo, flipping page after page, she recounted a rambling story of the day still fresh in her mind. In one photo, she posed in a stunning satin teal gown with a hand on her hip, flashing a proud grin at the camera. Next to her stood her prom date—a lanky, freckled, red-headed boy with a full set of braces.

"Isn't he hot?" She turned to me with bright eyes. "He's Robert. We're going out now."

Definitely not a Punjabi boy, I thought to myself. I looked at her, choked with feeling, and said, "Sorry I couldn't be there, Mina."

"No big deal. You would've been a drag anyway," she said, winking.

Mina sat across from me at the dinner table. The usual spot but with a new perspective, for we were no longer little girls but young women. The space next to me where Monika once sat was still empty. Her chair had been pushed back against the wall next to the window, furbished with a fancy cushion. I was dying to know about her and her new baby, whom she had named after me. An uneasy excitement lingered as the family gathered around the table. Mother circulated copper serving dishes and platters of rice and succulent chicken.

"I didn't put in a lot of oil," she said pointedly, as she held the rice platter over my clean unsoiled plate. "Say when."

"When!" I blurted almost immediately. She frowned at the scattering of rice on my dish. I raised my plate again and let her serve me another spoonful. I looked over at my dad and noticed that he had gotten trimmer. He sat taller and sturdier, his belly had flattened out, and his weathered complexion was replaced with a youthful sheen. Mother explained to me, as she served us, that her cooking had undergone a change. She had cut back on ghee, used less spices, and added more fresh herbs. I was convinced that my illness and hospitalization were what had caused her to become more conscientious of the health of her family. Cooking had always served to fill her hours of loneliness, but now seemed to be a source of pride and pleasure.

"Eat what you can, okay?" she said. Once the pressure was off, I could allow my taste buds to reacquaint themselves with the vibrant spices and juicy seasonings that I hadn't eaten in over a year. The flavours came alive on my palate and produced nervous excitement—and exceptional guilt. Another nibble slid off my spoon and into my mouth, a piquant and creamy morsel of meat under my tongue. The slippery grease coated my lips, causing me to perspire as I began to estimate the calories I'd consumed. I shuffled the peas around on my plate, unable to take in more. As Dad helped himself to another serving, I stopped him. "Take mine. I can't finish it."

He froze and looked at Mother. She nodded. I was relieved, but I could see a hint of concern in her eyes as she let out a deflated sigh.

"Mother, really, it was tasty ... I just"—my voice dropped—"I'm getting there."

"It's alright, Lila." She tapped my hand. "Next time, if you don't eat, I will redecorate your bedroom." Dad and Mina roared with laughter.

After dinner, I helped Mina and Mother with the dishes, while Dad wiped the table.

"How are Monika and her baby?" I asked, without looking up from the dish I was drying. I could feel Mother's movements slow down momentarily.

"They're fine," she said. "They've moved to Vancouver."

I put down the dish, stunned. "Why didn't anyone tell me?"

Mina brushed past me with a container and opened the fridge. "When did you ever bother to ask?"

Mother wiped her hands, reached for an envelope, and passed me some photos. "Here. Lila is almost two now."

Dad came over and shook off his rag in the sink. "And she's as stubborn as you are," he snickered. Monika had invited the family over on little Lila's first birthday, a few months after I was admitted to hospital. Since then, they had been in regular contact. I was stunned. Lila, the guileless little child, had charmed the entire family.

I realized, as I lay in bed that first night, that while I had been fighting time and age and life, my family had been embracing them with equal tenacity. A family, like any organism, seeks balance. It seeks to make up for the mad daughter and her belligerent disease.

I watched the curtain breathing, exhaling against the baseboard heater. The fabric danced as tremors of light from the street communicated secret symbols and cryptic messages for my hallucinating mind to decipher. As night crawled into the still depths of the morning, images slipped through the crack of the curtain, flickering onto the shades of my consciousness: Mina's shiny brown skin in the glimmering lake when we camped as kids; the sturdy nook of my father's shoulders where I rode so high I could touch heaven with my nose; the warm and tender flesh of my mother's arms. The curtain continued to breathe graciously as a ghostly breeze thrust inside it. It spread its lepidopteran wings into the room and possessed all my senses and obliterated my entire mind with the fullness of wonder. Those were my wings. They were full. They were strong. They were new.

Moments before the misty dawn of morning, I got up, took my Leica in my hands, and stood at the window with the camera's eye pointed to the uncertain day ahead. And I took flight.

Epilogue

Two weeks after the weekend pass, I was discharged from the hospital, never to return again. I continued therapy with Dr Bélanger as an out-patient for many years, and I continue to see her regularly.

Now I'm twenty-eight. I am slender, but I haven't been on a scale since I bid the hospital goodbye. My numerical weight doesn't reveal the big picture. According to the doctor, I'm healthy. I'm not suffering from any physical or mental disorder. There is no diagnosis. But my condition persists. It causes me to hold steadfast to my imagination, the prism of sensations, the marrow of feeling, the true and hidden world in between. I am a photographer. It's not just something I do for a living; it is a lifeline, the thing that keeps my heart beating, my lungs breathing, my wings fluttering.

Acknowledgments

I am indebted to the people who helped make this book happen: publisher Brian Lam, the editors Susan Safyan, Robyn So, and Linda Field. I would also like to acknowledge the continual support of my friend Kathy Adams, and of course the ongoing love and encouragement of my family, my father Harinder Marjara and sister Amita. Thanks to all of you.

EISHA MARJARA has written and directed several award-win-
ning films, including the critically acclaimed NFB docudrama
Desperately Seeking Helen, the witty and satirical *The Incredible
Shrinking Woman*, and the German-Canadian film *The Tour-
ist*. Her latest, *House for Sale*, has won numerous film festival
awards. *Faerie* is her first novel. She lives in Montreal.
eishamarjara.com